EMERS

SPIRITUAL GUIDE

A COMPANION TO

EMERSON'S ESSAYS

FOR PERSONAL REFLECTION
AND GROUP DISCUSSION

BARRY M. ANDREWS

SKINNER HOUSE BOOKS
BOSTON

DEDICATION

*To my sons, Ben and Aaron, who are a gift and a blessing.
"The power which resides in him is new in Nature,
and none but he knows what that is which he can do,
nor does he know until he has tried."*

Published by Skinner House Books. Skinner House Books is an imprint of
the Unitarian Universalist Association of Congregations, a liberal religious organization with more than 1,000 congregations in the U.S. and Canada. 25 Beacon
Street, Boston, MA 02108-2800.

Printed in Canada

ISBN 1-55896-449-5
978-1-55896-449-5

09 08 07
10 9 8 7 6 5 4 3 2

Cover design by Kimberly Glyder

Andrews, Barry Maxwell.
    Emerson as spiritual guide: a companion to selected essays of personal
reflections and group discussion/Barry M. Andrews.
        p.   cm.
    Includes bibliographical references.
    ISBN 1-55896-449-5 (alk. paper)
    1. Emerson, Ralph Waldo, 1803–1882—Religion. 2. Spiritual life in
literature. 3. Religion in literature. 4. Spiritual life. I. Title.

PS1642.R4A53 2003
814'.3—dc21

                                                                        2002044515

CONTENTS

INTRODUCTION

Two hundred years after his birth, Emerson continues to be a ubiquitous figure in American culture, easily the most recognized philosopher this country has produced. He was never a philosopher of the academic sort, but rather a popular philosopher—somewhat abstract, perhaps, but accessible. John Dewey called him "the Philosopher of Democracy" and went on to call him "the one citizen of the New World fit to have his name uttered in the same breath with that of Plato." In the eighty years since Dewey made those remarks, Emerson's reputation has waxed and waned, but today—his eminence enhanced by a generation of new scholarship—Emerson remains the quintessential American philosopher.

Indeed, it's hard to avoid him. As I drive to work in the morning, I pass the new wing of an elementary school, on the side of which is chiseled an Emerson quote. At the local grocery store, I pick up a box of easy-to-fix risotto with another of Emerson's sayings printed on the back: "For everything in nature contains all the powers of nature. Everything is made of one hidden stuff." Emerson was the master of aphorism and the most quotable of authors (so much so, in fact, that some of his most popular sayings were never said by him at all!) His quotations appear in greeting cards, commencement speeches, and newspaper columns and fill many pages of Bartlett's *Familiar Quotations*. No anthology of American literature is complete without selections from Emerson's essays and lectures.

As familiar a figure as Emerson is, it is notoriously difficult to classify him as a writer. He's a philosopher, to be sure. He's also a literary figure whose works are mostly found in the literature section of the local bookstore. Emerson is a great writer, but that accounts for only part of his appeal. The other labels often applied to him—poet, scholar, teacher, sage, mystic—are largely honorific. Emerson came from a long line of ministers and was educated to be a minister himself. Before he found success as a writer, Emerson served Boston's Second Unitarian Church, first as junior pastor and later as senior minister, for the better part of four years. Even after he resigned his pastorate at Second Church, he continued to preach for several years. Although Emerson made his reputation, not to say his living, as a lecturer on the lyceum circuit, more than one of his contemporaries felt he remained a preacher long after he traded his pulpit for a podium.

Certainly his lectures and essays contained spiritual and moral messages that had tremendous appeal to popular audiences. No one was more aware of the effect he had on others than Emerson himself. Friend and fellow Transcendentalist Elizabeth Peabody once heard him remark that his "special parish" was young men and women "inquiring their way of life." They looked to him, she said, for clues to living a spiritual life.

It's my belief that Emerson is first and foremost a spiritual writer and one of unusual depth and power. Those who ponder what he has to say will find that their own spiritual life has been stimulated and enriched. It is, therefore, as a spiritual guide that I approach Emerson in this companion to his essential writings.

If it is difficult to categorize Emerson as a writer, it's also hard to pigeonhole his ideas. Even today scholars try to trace the origin of his philosophy to various authors and schools of thought. But Emerson is not the sum of his sources. He read widely. He studied the classics of Eastern and Western philosophy and religion. He found inspiration in poetry and literature. He would have been the last to claim originality for his ideas and insights. But he did not derive his philosophy from his reading of Plato, Milton, Swedenborg, or the Hindu classics.

If anything, his studies revealed to him the perennial wisdom of philosophy and religion that was confirmed by his own experience and reflection. As he said in the opening words of "The Transcendentalist," "The first thing we have to say respecting what are called *new views* here in New England at the present time, is, that they are not new, but the very oldest of thoughts cast into the mould of these new times." As widely read as he was and as deeply steeped in religion and philosophy, Emerson relied first and foremost on his own experience. As he said often and in many ways, one must cultivate "an original relation to the universe," independent of the influence of others. Thus it's something of an irony to offer a guide to the writings of one who urged people to think for themselves.

The last thing Emerson wanted was followers. As he noted in his journal, "I have been writing and speaking what were once called novelties, for twenty five or thirty years, and have not now one disciple. Why? Not that what I said was not true; not that it has not found intelligent receivers, but because it did not go from any wish in me to bring men to me, but to themselves." Nevertheless, if he did not want to be anybody's guru, Emerson can at least be a guide, and we can seek to learn from his teaching and example. A great deal of his appeal has to do with his insistence that anyone might do as he did. Emerson championed a spiritual democracy, fully and freely available to all, without the mediation of priest or professor.

Today Emerson is more revered than read. In the adult education classes I teach on "Emerson as Spiritual Guide," I find that almost everyone has an anthology of Emerson's writings, but few have ever read more than one or two of the essays, usually "Self-Reliance" and "The Over-Soul." Nevertheless, these classes are generally well attended, and those who attend are eager to understand Emerson's philosophy, certain that there's wisdom in it for them.

The most frequent complaint I hear has to do with the difficulty of Emerson's language, which at times seems impenetrable. Reading Emerson can be a frustrating experience, especially for those who truly desire to understand him. His vocabulary is as extensive as it is unfamiliar. (What's a *firkin*, anyway?) Moreover, Emerson was a prodigious reader in an age of readers. Many of his allusions to classical literature, to philosophy and history, to religious scriptures, especially Eastern ones, to myth and fable are obscure even to the well-educated reader of today.

Besides the difficulty of understanding Emerson's vocabulary and references, there's the challenge of following his train of thought. By his own admission, Emerson was not a systematic thinker. Even in his day, people likened his arguments to a bird that flitted from branch to branch, and they often wondered what he was driving at.

But if Emerson is sometimes frustrating to read and if readers frequently need to reach for the dictionary, his turn of phrase, his metaphors, his juxtaposition of the earthy and the ethereal never cease to delight. Above all, his ideas are as exhilarating and as revolutionary as ever. The combination of great writing and profound thought is what keeps people coming back to him and why he's the most revered and quoted of American authors. Emerson is worth the effort.

My intention in offering this companion to Emerson's essays is to make them comprehensible in terms of their argument and the spiritual issues they raise today. Emerson considered it a sign of genius to believe that what's true for one's self is also true for others. Readers invariably feel a sense of comradeship when they recognize in Emerson a kindred soul and fellow seeker on the spiritual path. His writings read as though we are listening to Emerson think out loud. The essays covered in this volume deal most directly with religious and spiritual issues and reflect those concerns that Emerson considered most important in his own deeply spiritual life.

Reading is itself a spiritual discipline, a means of what Emerson termed self-culture. Emerson's writings yield insights to those who read them carefully and more than once. Perhaps these treatments of his essays and addresses can provide a useful map to what for many readers is unfamiliar territory and difficult terrain. They are arranged, more or less, in a chronological sequence, which reflects not only the range of his concerns, but also the way in which his thinking follows the trajectory of a long and, by turns, active and reflective life, from youthful idealism to what Emerson scholar David Robinson refers to as "the wisdom of experience." For one who said "a foolish consistency is the hobgoblin of little minds," Emerson's thinking remained remarkably constant. His ideas did grow and develop, and his focus shifted somewhat over time from an idealistic view of the world to a more pragmatic one. Even so, he never compromised the essentially revolutionary nature of his spiritual message. In this respect, he was a visionary to the end.

In what follows, I have endeavored to let Emerson speak for himself by quoting from him frequently. His profundity derives from his writing as much as his thinking. To paraphrase or recast his ideas in terms of a different vocabulary, academic or otherwise, is to lose the immediacy and urgency of his spiritual message. As a preacher and lecturer Emerson spoke directly to his audiences. As much as possible in a study guide such as this, I have tried to accord him the same privilege with his readers today.

The Summons to the Spiritual Life

On April 10, 1834, at the age of thirty-one, Ralph Waldo Emerson spent the afternoon at Mount Auburn Cemetery in Cambridge, Massachusetts. Even today, with its grassy knolls and green canopy of trees, Mount Auburn is an inviting place to visit. To be among the living in the silent company of the dead is inevitably to find oneself in a contemplative frame of mind. Writing in his journal the next day, Emerson described his experience:

> I forsook the tombs, and found a sunny hollow where the east wind would not blow, and lay down against the side of a tree to most happy beholdings. At least I opened my eyes and let what would pass through them into the soul. I saw no more my relation, how near and petty, to Cambridge or Boston; I heeded no more what minute or hour our Massachusetts clocks might indicate—I only saw the noble earth on which I was born, with the great Star which warms and enlightens it. I saw the clouds that hang their significant drapery over us. It was Day—that was all Heaven said. The pines glittered with their innumerable green needles in the light, and seemed to challenge me to read their riddle. The drab oak-leaves of the last year turned their little somersets and lay still again. And the wind bustled high overheard in the forest top. This gay and grand architecture, from the vault to the moss and lichen on which I lay—who shall explain to me the laws of its proportions and adornments?

Emerson had a lot of time on his hands during this period of his life and much to think about. Three years earlier, his young wife, Ellen, had died of tuberculosis, leaving him totally bereft. Shortly afterward, he resigned his pulpit at Second Church in Boston, in large part because he felt he could not in good conscience continue to serve the Lord's Supper. Despondent, alienated from his profession, and forever separated from the one he loved, he set sail for Europe. He was gone for ten months. Bound for home, he confided in his journal, "I . . . wish I knew where and how I ought to live."

The months following his return were filled with soul-searching. He felt he was in limbo, caught between a past that was closed to him and a future he could not yet see. At the same time he had an awareness that a vast universe of possibilities awaiting realization was all around him. "We stand on the edge of all that is great," he wrote in his journal, "yet are restrained in inactivity and unconscious of our powers. We are always on the brink of an ocean of thought into which we do not yet swim."

"Much preparation, little fruit," he continued. "But suddenly in any place, in the street, in the chamber, will the heavens open and the regions of wisdom be uncovered, as if to show how thin the veil, how null the circumstances. As quickly, a stream [of forgetfulness] washes through us and bereaves us of ourselves." Then, in a passage underlined for emphasis, he writes these seminal words: "What a benefit if a rule could be given whereby the mind, dreaming amid the gross fogs of matter, could at any moment *east itself* and *find the sun!*"

This is a breakthrough moment for Emerson, and this sentence becomes the defining task and central message of his philosophy. It's also the most persistent and perennial question we face in our own spiritual lives. Like Emerson, we know we stand on the brink of the infinite—call it God, call it Spirit, call it the Void even. It's a source of incredible power and energy, capable of gilding our ordinary lives with meaning and significance. We sense its presence, and sometimes unexpectedly the heavens open and the regions of wisdom are revealed. But the experience soon fades, and we revert to our accustomed ways.

All of us have had experiences similar to what Emerson described, moments saturated with meaning, times when we have felt especially alive and aware and at one with the universe. Such experiences may come at any time and in any place—in the chamber or in the street, as Emerson says, or even in a cemetery. They may come unexpectedly or at the end of a long period of preparation. They may come as flashing insights into the nature of Reality or subtle inklings and intuitions of something beyond, something larger than ourselves.

A few days after his experience at Mount Auburn, Emerson noted in his journal that people desire to be awake. "Get the soul out of bed, out of her deep habitual sleep," he wrote, "out into God's universe, to a perception of its beauty, and hearing of its call," and one becomes "a god, and is conscious of force to shake the world." When we have such experiences, we feel alive and strangely powerful. But given the fact that these experiences fade, what are we to do?

In virtually everything he said and wrote, Emerson was wrestling with the two most important issues concerning the spiritual life: How do we recapture or continue to benefit from these moments? How do we live during the times between them? These moments represent the high points of our lives, times when we live with greater intensity and passion, when we feel deeply connected with others and with the forces of the universe. They are intuitions of the nature of things, glimpses of unlimited possibilities, and visions of a life transformed.

The mundane tasks of everyday existence seem to stand in sharp contrast to such moments. The realities of life include grocery shopping, tedious meetings, rebellious teenagers, marital problems, and periods of depression as well as infrequent times of ecstasy and bliss. Much of contemporary culture is inimical to living life on a higher plane, and ours is a very materialistic society, based, in Emerson's view, on "the lucrative standard."

Maybe we should just forget about it and go on with our business. Life is already difficult. But try as we might to ignore its call, the universe continues to beckon us. We live, after all, in a world of incredible beauty, and reminders of the wonder and mystery of life are everywhere. Sometimes we are overwhelmed, as when we witness the birth of a child or the death of a loved one. Sometimes we are simply caught off guard, as when the sunlight catches the trees in the late afternoon. There's a deep-seated longing to feel connected with the *sacred,* which is simply a term we use to describe this sense of mystery and wonder. We have a hunger for wholeness, a feeling that we are being reminded of something we once knew.

The summons to the spiritual life may occur in many ways. For Emerson it was precipitated by a series of traumatic experiences: the death of his young wife, a debilitating illness, and a crisis of faith that led to his departure from the ministry. Suffering and loss are powerful teachers. Some people succumb to these experiences, while others struggle to make sense of them and put them into some sort of perspective.

The call often seems like a search for something that has been lost, as is suggested in this enigmatic passage from Henry David Thoreau's *Walden*:

> I long ago lost a hound, a bay horse and a turtle-dove, and am still on
> their trail. Many are the travelers I have spoken concerning them,
> describing their tracks and what calls they answered to. I have met
> one or two who had heard the hound, and the tramp of the horse,
> and even seen the dove disappear behind a cloud, and they seemed
> as anxious to recover them as if they had lost them themselves.

The sighting of the tracks or the fleeting glimpse of the sacred, as Thoreau describes it, is a summons to awakening. If spirituality is a search for something lost, what must we do to find it again? Essentially two things according to Emerson: Follow a practice and develop a certain kind of wisdom.

To have a longing for the sacred isn't enough; we need a vessel or a practice to carry us on the journey, to take us from where we are to where we want to be. The great spiritual traditions offer choices in this regard. The teachings of the Buddha are said to be a raft. The Transcendentalists, of whom Emerson was the guiding figure, developed a spiritual practice that consisted of contemplation, reading, journal writing, and sauntering in the out-of-doors. In following such a practice the Transcendentalists were not markedly different from spiritual seekers in other traditions.

The goal of the spiritual life is to open us up to the reality that exists all around us. We are cut off from it by layers of egotism, pain, fear, anger, and judgment. We also live in a culture that is not conducive to the needs of the spirit. The frenetic pace of everyday life leaves us feeling restless and anxious. A spiritual practice allows us to quiet ourselves enough to listen to the voices within and to hear the rustling of the spirit in the world around us. Contemplation enables us to step outside of our usual roles, outside of days spent on automatic pilot. Like Emerson in the graveyard, we need to find a way to become open to the oneness of the universe.

The wisdom Emerson sought to teach is alluded to by the contemporary author Robert Fulghum, who found, after a period of study at a Zen Buddhist monastery in Japan, that he had been "a thirsty man looking for a drink while standing knee-deep in a flowing stream." Wisdom does not consist of knowledge. It consists of the realization that, more than knee-deep, we are literally immersed in a gracious reality, nourished by the sun and the rain and the fertile earth, embraced in the great mystery of life. With wisdom and practice we can return to daily existence knowing that the spiritual life consists of the mundane as well as the mystical and that wherever we are in this world of peaks and valleys, we are at home. In the course of a long and productive life, Ralph Waldo Emerson discovered that enlightenment is not an end result but an ongoing process of self-transformation or spiritual growth.

His basic message was not a complicated one, any more than that of other great spiritual teachers, including Jesus and the Buddha. The difficulty consists in hearing and heeding that message amid the distractions of a world seemingly indifferent to spiritual renewal and the cultivation of the soul.

I believe that Americans today are yearning for a deeper spiritual life. Bookstores and talk shows are a testament to the burgeoning interest in spiritual matters. Many people today feel, as Emerson sometimes did himself, that "life is superficial, [and] takes no root in the deep world." In a major study of the religious life of post–World War II Americans, *Spiritual Marketplace,* sociologist Wade Clark Roof came to the following conclusion:

> Three aspects of the situation today particularly stand out. One is the sheer numbers of people involved: spiritual searching is hardly limited to a few bold spirits, to either marginalized or privileged classes.

Surveys show that large sectors of the American population today are interested in deepening their spirituality. Many who seem to have lost a traditional religious grounding are striving for new and fresh moorings; many with a religious grounding are looking to enrich their lives further. Second, dominant amid all this ferment is an emphasis on self-understanding and self-reflexivity, a product of late modernity with its pluralism, relativism, and ontological uncertainties. . . . Third, and somewhat paradoxically, the spiritual yearnings are leading many Americans beyond the self-centered, therapeutic culture in which they grew up. Self-fulfillment as a cultural theme in the 1960s and 1970s set in motion a powerful quest, but now for a generation older and more mature that quest has moved beyond the solutions that were promised in consumption, materialism and self-absorption. Popular spirituality may appear shallow, indeed flaky; yet its creative currents, under the right conditions, can activate our deepest energies and commitments. Even in its most self-absorbed forms, today's spiritual ferment reflects a deep hunger for a self-transformation that is both genuine and personally satisfying.

In Roof's interviews the words *quest, seeking,* and *searching* are most often used to characterize the nature of the religious life of the nation's baby-boom generation. From his perspective he sees that "a set of social and cultural transformations have created a quest culture, a search for certainty, but also the hope for a more authentic, intrinsically satisfying life." Ralph Waldo Emerson is the patron saint of religious seekers. Indeed, he described himself as "an endless seeker, with no Past at my back." His insistence that conscience is a reliable guide in ethical decision making provides an anchor in a world of moral relativism. And his teaching on self-reliance is the key to living "a more authentic, intrinsically satisfying life."

In another study of religious life in America since the 1950s, Robert Wuthnow observes that with skepticism and a loss of faith in doctrines and religious institutions, Americans have adopted "a new spirituality of seeking" as a means of acquiring spiritual knowledge and practical wisdom. Like Emerson, people today increasingly distinguish between religion and spirituality. For Emerson, as for many contemporary Americans, skepticism and religious formalism have undercut the foundations of faith. When Emerson says, in his characteristically provocative way, "God builds his temple in the human heart on the ruins of churches and religions," he articulates a sentiment felt by many in his day and ours.

However, Emerson's seeking was not an aimless meandering. It was a disciplined quest for *self-culture*, what we might call the cultivation of the soul. It was guided by a spiritual practice that consisted of contemplation, journal writing, conversation, reading, and an appreciation of nature. Wuthnow argues that there's a difference between seeker-oriented spirituality and practice-oriented spirituality. Seeker-oriented spirituality allows people to find their own way and take advantage of a variety of opportunities for developing their own synthesis of religion and spirituality. Unfortunately, in Wuthnow's view, it often "results in a transient spiritual existence characterized more often by dabbling than by depth."

On the other hand, practice-oriented spirituality utilizes activities, referred to as disciplines, as a means of establishing a connection to or relationship with reality or the sacred. It's a more focused and directed form of spirituality, often associated with a particular religious tradition or community of faith. As Wuthnow puts it, "the idea of spiritual practices encourages individuals to take responsibility for their own spiritual development by spending time working on it, deliberating on its meaning and how best to pursue it, seeking to understand the sacred through reading and the counsel of others, and seeking to have contact with the sacred through personal reflection and prayer."

Emerson's teaching is a synthesis of both of these forms of spirituality. It is rooted in a broadly Unitarian tradition, itself a synthesis drawing from many sources and promoting a seeker-oriented form of spirituality within the context of religious community. Emerson's emphasis on self-culture provides a means and a mind-set for developing and pursuing intentional ways of seeking contact with reality and of relating one's life to it. His teaching offers to thoughtful spiritual practitioners a means of attaining spiritual knowledge and practical wisdom for life, even, perhaps especially, for Americans struggling with the everyday realities and moral complexities of the twenty-first century.

The Spiritual Vision of Ralph Waldo Emerson

"There is a difference between one and another hour of life in their authority and subsequent effect," Emerson writes in "The Over-Soul." "Our faith comes in moments; our vice is habitual. Yet there is more depth in those brief moments which constrains us to ascribe more reality to them than all other experiences." Who hasn't experienced such moments? Who hasn't assigned more authority to them than to everyday experiences? Who hasn't longed to hold on to them in hopes of living a richer, fuller life?

Emerson made it his mission to discern and delineate the promptings of these experiences. As he notes in his journal, "I am to indicate, though all unworthy, the Ideal and Holy Life, the life within life, the Forgotten Good, the Unknown Cause in which we sprawl and sin. I am to celebrate the spiritual powers in their infinite contrast to the mechanical powers and the mechanical philosophy of this time." He later describes himself as "a professor of the Joyous Science, a detector and delineator of occult harmonies and unpublished beauties, a herald of civility, nobility, learning, and wisdom; an affirmer of the One Law, yet as one who should affirm it in music or dancing, a priest of the Soul."

Emerson was determined not to stint or compromise in his attempt to detect and describe these "occult harmonies and unpublished beauties." Except for a few notable travelers who preceded him—Jesus, the Buddha, and mystics, among others—Emerson was venturing into unknown territory. He was not always certain he was up to the task. He experienced keenly the contradictions or polarities of the spiritual life, one of which he describes in his journal:

> A certain wandering light comes to me which I instantly perceive to be the Cause of Causes. It transcends all proving. It is itself the ground of being; and I see that it is not one and I another, but this is the life of my life. That is one fact, then; that in certain moments I have known that I existed directly from God, and am, as it were, God's organ. And in my ultimate consciousness Am God. Then, secondly, the contradictory fact is familiar, that I am a surprised spectator and learner of all my life. This is the habitual posture of the mind—beholding. But whenever the day dawns, the great day of truth on the soul, it comes with awful invitation to me to accept it, to blend with its aurora. Cannot I conceive the Universe without a contradiction?

Clearly, Emerson was caught between the desire to lose himself in the ecstasy of the moment ("to blend with its aurora") and to be an observer, on the outside looking in (his "habitual posture of the mind"). He describes this condition as the dilemma of "double consciousness." Although he may never have succeeded in reconciling this dilemma to his satisfaction, it was Emerson's intention to demonstrate in his life and writings what "the Universe without a contradiction" might look like.

Genius, according to Emerson, is the quality of allowing the spirit to have its way with us. It was a quality that he highly prized. Those whom he admired—heroes, poets, saints, and sages—were those who demonstrated genius in this way. We think of genius as extraordinary talent or intelligence. Emerson felt that all people possess genius. Paradoxically, it makes them at once unique and identical because the genius in each is the genius in all, though it manifests itself differently in every individual as a personal calling or gift. Genius, he says in "The Over-Soul," is "a larger imbibing of the common heart. It is not anomalous, but more like and not less like other men."

This is why Emerson insists, as in "Self-Reliance," that "to believe your own thought, to believe that what is true for you is true for all

men,—that is genius." Contrary to what many of his critics have right
believed, self-reliance doesn't mean unbridled individualism. In
Emerson's view as recorded in his journal, "More genius does not
increase the *individuality*, but the *community* of each mind." What
we find remarkable in Shakespeare, for instance, is not how alien he
is from us, but how alike; how, in expressing his individuality as a
writer, he speaks for us also.

Genius is the prompting of the soul, common to all, embodied in
each. When we respond to our genius, we are carried like a kite in the
wind into the upper atmosphere of the spiritual life. The soul is not
a being, but Being itself; it's not an object, but a force or power. This
larger, universal soul—the over-soul—corresponds to the soul in
each individual. The relationship between the two is described in a
memorable passage from "The Over-Soul":

> All goes to show that the soul in man is not an organ, but animates
> and exercises all the organs; is not a function, like the power of
> memory, of calculation, of comparison, but uses these as hands and
> feet; is not a faculty, but a light; is not the intellect or the will, but the
> master of the intellect and the will; is the background of our being,
> in which they lie,—an immensity not possessed and that cannot be
> possessed. From within or from behind, a light shines through us
> upon things, and makes us aware that we are nothing, but the light
> is all. . . . When it breathes through his intellect, it is genius; when it
> breathes through his will, it is virtue; when it flows through his affec-
> tion, it is love. . . . All reform aims, in some one particular, to let the
> soul have its way through us; in other words, to engage us to obey.

In this same essay, Emerson notes that this energy, though available to all, "does not descend into individual life on any other condition than entire possession." The promise of this influx of genius
is the reunification of a divided life. But it can be achieved only
through self-trust and courage. It's another of the paradoxes of the
spiritual life that in order to save one's life, one must lose it; that is,
one must let go, just as the apple must let go of the tree if it is to
become a tree itself. What the natural world does by instinct, human
beings must do consciously. But humans hesitate. Therefore, we
must have trust in the self or soul, and we must have courage, not

11

merely to let go, though this requires courage enough, but to endure the disapproval of those who view self-reliance as an invitation to licentiousness or to irresponsibility.

As Emerson knew from the criticism he received, those who can't trust themselves can't trust others either. On this particular score, Unitarian minister Theodore Parker, Emerson's contemporary and fellow Transcendentalist, wrote of him in *The Massachusetts Quarterly Review* that

> few men in America have been visited with more hatred,—private personal hatred, which the authors poorly endeavored to conceal, and perhaps did hide from themselves. The spite we have heard expressed against him, by men of the common morality, would strike a stranger with amazement, especially when it is remembered that his personal character and daily life are of such extraordinary loveliness.

Even today, Emerson is attacked by critics with the condescending attitude that ordinary people can't be trusted with such dangerous ideas.

Indeed, as Emerson argues in "Self-Reliance," all too often people heed these criticisms. We should learn "to detect and watch that gleam of light" that flashes across our minds from within. But we dismiss such thoughts because they are ours. The voices we hear in solitude grow faint and inaudible as we enter into the world. Society conspires against individuality. "The virtue in most request is conformity. Self-reliance is its aversion." As for the criticism that the voices we hear might be from the devil, Emerson offers this rejoinder:

> What I must do is all that concerns me, not what people think. This rule, equally arduous in actual and intellectual life, may serve for the whole distinction between greatness and meanness. It is the harder because you will always find those who think they know what is your duty better than you know it. It is easy to live after the world's opinion; it is easy in solitude to live after our own; but the great man is he who in the midst of the crowd keeps with perfect sweetness the independence of solitude.

How often have we stifled our thoughts and feelings and failed to heed the promptings of our hearts? For that matter, how much stock does society put in solitude? And where, in the busy lives we lead, do we find the time for it? As Emerson well knew, society has more champions than solitude. But it's only in solitude that we become aware that we are not separate, isolated individuals, but that we "share the life by which all things exist." In solitude we discover that we "lie in the lap of immense intelligence, which makes us receivers of its truth and organs of its activity."

In "The Over-Soul," Emerson describes this perception as an influx of the Divine mind into our mind:

> It is an ebb of the individual rivulet before the flowing surges of the sea of life. Every distinct apprehension of this distinct command-ment agitates men with awe and delight. . . . Every moment when the individual feels himself invaded by it is memorable. By the necessity of our constitution a certain enthusiasm attends the individual's con-sciousness of that divine presence. The character and duration of this enthusiasm vary with the state of the individual, from an ecstasy and trance and prophetic inspiration—which is its rarer appearance—to the faintest glow of virtuous emotion, in which form it warms, like our household fires, all the families and associations of men, and makes society possible.

These experiences are, as Emerson suggests, spontaneous, ecstatic, and evanescent. They are at once ineffable and full of significance. It's as though we are spoken to from behind, unable to see the face of the speaker. "That well known voice speaks in all languages, governs all men, and none ever caught a glimpse of its form," Emerson writes in "The Method of Nature." But if we will obey that voice, it will adopt us and we will no longer be divided within ourselves, richer and greater wisdom will be ours, we will become careless of food and home, and lead a heavenly life. But if we are preoccupied with everyday tasks, "then the voice grows faint." Our health and greatness consists in being "the channel through which heaven flows to earth, in short in the fullness in which an ecstatical state" takes place in us.

These experiences are not only ecstatic; they provide insights into the nature of reality itself. In a fragment of a letter to his brother Edward—quoted in his journal—Emerson writes, "Much of what we learn, and to the highest purposes, of life is caught in moments, and rather by a sublime instinct than by modes that can be explained in detail." This distinction is also described as the difference between reason and understanding. For Emerson, reason is an intuitive faculty, while understanding is a rational, intellectual process. He explains what he means by these terms in another letter to Edward:

> Reason is the highest faculty of the soul, what we mean by the soul itself; it never reasons, never proves; it simply perceives, it is vision. The Understanding toils all the time, compares, contrives, adds, argues; near-sighted, dwelling in the present, the expedient, the customary.

Emerson identified understanding with intellect and reason with intuition, and argued that it was through the latter that we have access to the realm of the spirit.

What Emerson learned intuitively was that the world is an outgrowth of the universal mind, or oversoul. God, in Emerson's use of the term, is not a being separate and apart from the world. God is immanent, not transcendent. God is the substratum of all things. "What is God," he asks in his journal, "but the name of the Soul at the center by which all things are what they are?" As far as human beings are concerned, God is within. "As long as the soul seeks an external God, it never can have peace," he insists. "It always must be uncertain what may be done and what may become of it. But when it sees the Great God far within its own nature, then it sees that always itself is a party to all that can be, that always it will be informed of that which will happen and therefore it is pervaded with a great Peace."

Emerson denied personality to God because, as he wrote in his journal, "it is too little not too much." Indeed, for all his ingenious turns of phrase, he concluded that God was essentially beyond words: "Of that ineffable essence which we call Spirit," he wrote in *Nature*, "he that thinks most, will say the least. We can foresee God in the course and, as it were, distant phenomena of matter; but when we try to define and describe [God] both language and thought desert us and we are as helpless as fools and savages." The language that he did use, inadequate though he may have felt it to be, suggests that God is an intelligent, albeit impersonal, force. In Emerson's experience, God is dynamic and progressive. God is variously described as ecstasy, "vast-flowing vigor," ("Experience") and, in a particularly favorite phrase, "the flying Perfect, around which the hands of man can never meet, at once the inspirer and the condemner of every success" ("Circles").

The natural world, which is a manifestation or embodiment of God, shares these qualities. "There are no fixtures in nature," Emerson insists in "Circles." "The universe is fluid and volatile. Permanence is but a world of degrees." Nature, like God, is ecstatic. It's a "rushing stream [that] will not stop to be observed." Emerson tells us in "The Method of Nature,"

> We can never surprise nature in a corner; never find the end of a thread; never tell where to set the first stone. The bird hastens to lay her egg: the egg hastens to be a bird. The wholeness we admire in the order of the world, is the result of infinite distribution. Its smoothness is the smoothness of the pitch of the cataract. Its permanence is a perpetual inchoation. Every natural fact is an emanation, and that from which it emanates is an emanation also, and from every emanation is a new emanation. If anything could stand still, it would be crushed and dissipated by the torrent it resisted, and if it were a mind, would be crazed; as insane persons are those who hold fast to one thought, and do not flow with the course of nature.

Human beings are part and parcel of nature. As creatures of this world and emanations of God, we are provided for. Emerson notes in his journal, "The good Earth, the planet on which we are embarked and making our annual voyage in the unharboured Deep carries in her bosom every good thing her children need on the way for refreshment, fuel, science, or action. She has coal in the hold and all meats in the larder and is overhung with showiest awning." But there are no special privileges for us as individuals or as a species. Nature "does not exist to any one or to any number of particular ends, but to numberless and endless benefit." Emerson observes in "The Method of Nature" that "there is in it no private will, no rebel leaf or limb, but the whole . . . obeys that redundancy or excess of life which in conscious beings we call *ecstasy*."

If human beings are not privileged in Emerson's universe, they do have a special destiny; namely, "to lead things from disorder into order." Each soul shares the attributes of God "in virtue of its being a power to translate the world into some particular language of its own; if not into a picture, a statue, or a dance—why, then, into a trade, an art, a science, a mode of living, a conversation, a character, an influence." Every person has a purpose, a mission, or a vocation in life, something he or she is uniquely qualified to do. At the same time, we each possess an unlimited potential to accomplish it.

Success in life consists of discerning and pursuing one's unique calling, of "following one's bliss," in Joseph Campbell's memorable phrase. "Each man has his own vocation," Emerson writes in "Spiritual Laws,"

> The talent is the call. There is one direction in which all space is open to him. He has faculties silently inviting him thither to endless exertion. He is like a ship in a river; he runs against obstructions on every side but one; on that side all obstruction is taken away, and he sweeps serenely over a deepening channel into an infinite sea. This talent and this call depend on his organization, or the mode in which the general soul incarnates itself in him. . . . His ambition is exactly proportioned to his powers. The height of the pinnacle is determined by the breadth of the base. Every man has this call of the power to do somewhat unique, and no man has any other call.

We are baulked whenever we attempt to go against the grain or current of nature. A higher law than our will regulates events, such that "our painful labors are unnecessary and fruitless; that only in our simple, spontaneous action are we strong." Self-trust is the key:

> The whole course of things goes to teach us faith. We need only obey. There is guidance for each of us, and by lowly listening we shall hear the right word. Why need you choose so painfully your place, and occupation, and associates, and modes of action, and of entertainment? Certainly there is a possible right for you that precludes the need of balance and wilful election. For you there is a reality, a fit place and congenial duties. Place yourself in the middle of the stream of power and wisdom which animates all whom it floats, and you are without effort impelled to truth, to right, and a perfect contentment.

Unfortunately, as Emerson puts it in "The Natural History of Intellect," the "history of mankind" is the "history of arrested growth." It appears that most people come to a premature stop, not realizing that, like nature itself, they are made for action, not rest. It's only in action, by throwing ourselves into the fray, that we have power and greatness. Nothing significant was ever accomplished by the timid. The problem, as Emerson describes it in "Lecture on the Times," is that for the better part of our lives we simply drift,

> white sail across the wild ocean, now bright on the wave, now darkling in the trough of the sea;—but from what port did we sail? Who knows? Or to what port are we bound? Who knows? There is no one to tell us but such weather-tossed mariners as ourselves, whom we speak as we pass, or who have hoisted some signal, or floated to us some letter in a bottle from far. But what know they more than we?

We all find ourselves adrift on "this wondrous sea," but we do not realize that the answer to the question of where we are bound is in ourselves, in "the intuitions which are vouchsafed us from within." We assume that life is merely ashes to ashes and dust to dust, not realizing that there's immortality for us in the Eternal Now. "Underneath all these appearances, lies that which lives, that which causes. This ever renewing generation of appearances rests on a reality, and a reality that is alive."

Emerson was painfully aware of the difficulty of living such a life. "The Transcendentalist," he says in "The Transcendentalist," "adopts the whole connection of spiritual doctrine. He believes in miracle, in the perpetual openness of the human mind to new influx of light and power, he believes in inspiration, and in ecstasy." Yet he was forced to admit that while "we have had many harbingers and forerunners of a spiritual life," none have thus far succeeded.

> I mean, we have yet no man who has leaned entirely on his character, and eaten angels' food; who, trusting to his sentiments, found life made of miracles; who, working for universal aims, found himself fed, he knew not how; clothed, sheltered, and weaponed, he knew not how, and yet it was done by his own hands. Only in the instinct of the lower animals, we find the suggestion of the methods

of it, and something higher than our understanding. The squirrel hoards nuts, and the bee gathers honey, without knowing what they do, and they are thus provided for without selfishness or disgrace.

What animals do by instinct, human beings must do consciously. Thus we encounter one of the perennial paradoxes of the spiritual life: the contradiction involved in willing to do something that requires a surrender of the will. If Emerson was not able to resolve this dilemma to his own satisfaction, he was able to provide in his life and writings a model and guidebook for others who make the effort to do so.

A GOD IN RUINS

The Paradox of the Spiritual Life

Emerson writes in his journal, "I remember when I was a boy going upon the beach and being charmed with the colors and forms of the shells. I picked up many and put them in my pocket. When I got home I could find nothing that I had gathered—nothing but some dry ugly mussel and snail shells." It's not an uncommon experience. We gather stones and shells at the seaside, attracted by their shape and luster, only to find them dull and ordinary once we get them home. At the seashore—as in any natural surrounding—our perceptions are enhanced and the world assumes a grace and grandeur we wish we could carry with us into our ordinary existence. But it's not the stones or shells that become dull in the light of home. The dullness of everyday life makes them appear so. In other words, the problem is not the in the shells themselves, but in our perception.

The difference between the shells on the beach and the ones at home is the difference between the *real* and the *actual*. People think that what's spiritual is invisible, says Emerson, but the "true meaning of *spiritual* is real." The spiritual stands in contrast not to the real, but to the actual, that is, to the material. The material—the actual—is the realm of understanding. It is preoccupied with practical matters, with facts and figures, with getting a living and maintaining appearances. Whereas the spiritual—the real—is the realm of reason. It is concerned with quality rather than quantity, with essences rather than appearances, with the depth of life rather than its surface.

The problem is that we spend the better part of our lives living in the actual world when it's reality that we desire. The material so predominates that the spiritual is overlaid and lost. "Let it be granted, that our life, as we lead it, is common and mean," says Emerson in "Man the Reformer," "that the community in which we live will hardly bear to be told that every man should be open to ecstasy or a divine illumination, and his daily walk elevated by intercourse with the spiritual world." Without a sense of depth in life, our existence is shallow and superficial. We become selfish members of a selfish society, judging everything by "the lucrative standard." We enjoy every convenience, "ride four times as fast as our fathers did; travel, grind, weave, forge, plant, till and excavate better," Emerson reminds us in "Works and Days." We have consumer goods, science and technology, and mass media. "Much will have more. Man flatters himself that his command over Nature must increase." Indeed, our appetite appears to be insatiable. Emerson invokes the mythical figure of Tantalus to describe our hunger:

> Tantalus, who in old times was seen vainly trying to quench his thirst with a flowing stream which ebbed whenever he approached it, has been seen again lately. He is in Paris, in New York, in Boston. He is now in great spirits; thinks he shall reach it yet; thinks he shall bottle the wave. It is however getting a little doubtful. . . . No matter how many centuries of culture have preceded, the new man always finds himself standing on the brink of chaos, always in crisis.

Our yearning after material goods and sensual pleasures can bring no satisfaction. Emerson observes in "Worship" that there is "no bond, no fellow-feeling, no enthusiasm" in our cities. People are not persons, "but hungers, thirsts, fevers, and appetites walking. How is it [they] manage to live on, so aimless as they are?" We have "faith in chemistry, in meat, and wine, in wealth, in machinery, in the steam-engine, galvanic battery, turbine wheels, sewing machines, and in public opinion, but not in divine causes." And so we are trapped in skepticism and self-doubt. We grope for stays and foundations, but find none. Skepticism devastates community. But it can't be arrested or cured by any modification of religious creeds or practices. "God builds his temple in the heart," he says, "on the ruins of churches and religions."

Skepticism, because it undermines confidence and certainty, leads to feelings of ennui and aimlessness. Lacking a sense of transcendence, we are trapped in the world of experience. "Where do we find ourselves?" Emerson asks. In a memorable passage from his essay "Experience," he describes the spiritual lethargy that follows in the wake of skepticism:

> We wake and find ourselves on a stair; there are stairs below us, which we seem to have ascended; there are stairs above us, many a one, which go upward and out of sight. But the Genius which, according to the old belief, stands at the door by which we enter, and gives us the lethe to drink, that we may tell no tales, mixed the cup too strongly, and we cannot shake off the lethargy now at noonday. Sleep lingers all our lifetime about our eyes, as night hovers all day in the boughs of the fir-tree. All things swim and glitter. Our life is not so much threatened as our perception. Ghostlike we glide through nature, and should not know our place again . . . it appears to us that we lack the affirmative principle, and though we have health and reason, yet we have no superfluity of spirit for new creation. We have enough to live and bring the year about, but not an ounce to impart or to invest. . . . We are like millers on the lower levels of a stream, when the factories above them have exhausted the water.

Besides materialism, skepticism, and ennui, we are prey to the snares of illusion. Lacking a taste of "the real quality of existence," we are trapped in the world of appearances. "There are as many pillows of illusion as flakes in a snow-storm," Emerson observes in "Illusions." "We wake from one dream into another dream. The toys, to be sure are various, and are graduated in refinement to the quality of the dupe. The intellectual man requires a fine bait; the sots are easily amused. But everybody is drugged with his own frenzy, and the pageant marches at all hours, with music and banner and badge." Occasionally, however, as Emerson describes in "Illusions," we are afforded a glimpse of the reality behind these appearances:

> From day to day, the capital facts of human life are hidden from our eyes. Suddenly the mist rolls up, and reveals them, and we think how much good time is gone, that might have been saved, had any hint of

these things been shown. A sudden rise in the road shows us the system of mountains, and all the summits, which have been just as near us all the year, but quite out of mind.

Society and the routines of daily living are sadly at odds with the vast potential of the human personality. Emerson describes mankind in Nature as distrustful, bereft of reason, "a god in ruins." We apply to life but half our force. We work on the world with our understanding alone. We live in it and master it by "a penny-wisdom." In *Nature*, the first of his many books, Emerson identifies the solution to what he has termed the "problem of double-consciousness":

> The problem of restoring to the world original and eternal beauty is solved by the redemption of the soul. The ruin or blank that we see when we look at nature, is in our own eye. The axis of vision is not coincident with the axis of things, and so they appear not transparent, but opaque. The reason why the world lacks unity, and lies broken and in heaps, is because we are disunited within ourselves.

What he means is that we need to strike a balance between reason and understanding, insight and intellect, a balance that doesn't currently exist. If we are to redeem the soul and thereby strike that balance, we must alter or cleanse our perceptions. The ruin or blank we see is in our own eye. The mist that hides "the capital facts of human life" from view is in our own mind. "That only which we have within, can we see without," Emerson asserts in "Worship." "If we meet no gods, it is because we harbor none."

How do we strike this balance? How do we alter or cleanse our perceptions? Emerson sought to answer these questions for himself. His journal is a record of his experiments and conclusions. In an entry dated April 1834, he makes the following observation:

> We are always getting ready to live, but never living. We have many years of technical education; then, many years of earning a livelihood, and we get sick, and take journeys for our health, and compass land and sea for improvement by travelling, but the work of self-improvement—always under the nose—nearer than the nearest, is seldom engaged in. A few, few hours in the longest life.

Set out to study a particular truth. Read upon it. Walk to think upon it. Talk of it. Write about it. The thing itself will not much manifest itself, at least not much in accommodation to your studying arrangements. The gleams you do get, out they will flash, as likely at dinner, or in the roar of Faneuil Hall, as in your painfullest abstraction.

Very little life in a lifetime.

In this passage we see the rudiments of what Emerson referred to as self-culture, the cultivation or nurture of the soul. The self that is to be improved here is not the ego or the intellect; it's the reason or the soul.

The spiritual life is characterized by several paradoxes. The first is the one just mentioned, the problem of double consciousness, which Emerson alludes to in so many of his writings. It's best captured in the opening lines of "The Over-Soul": "Our faith comes in moments; our vice is habitual. Yet there is more depth in those brief moments which constrains us to ascribe more reality to them than all other experiences." This is the difference between what's real and what's actual. It's the actual world we live in, but it's reality we seek. The dilemma is complicated by the fact that these are not two separate worlds; they are one and the same. It's our perception or mode of consciousness that accounts for the difference between the two.

The second major paradox has to do with the method of cultivating experiences of reality. It would appear to be a contradiction to suggest that such experiences could be summoned at will. In the first place, they seem to come unannounced and unbidden. And if they could be evoked, there would be no paradox or problem of double consciousness. Moreover, the lesson these experiences teach is letting go, acquiescence, and surrender of the will. How can one summon and surrender simultaneously? Zen describes this paradox as akin to trying to grab a fistful of water. The late Alan Watts likened it to the futility of raising oneself by one's own bootstraps.

Emerson wrestled with this problem during the whole course of his life, though he seemed to resolve it differently as time went on. These two modes of consciousness reflect a principle that Emerson describes in "The American Scholar" as "deeply ingrained in every atom and every fluid, . . . known to us as Polarity." But in Emerson's view, they are complementary, not mutually exclusive. Each is half of a whole. They are variously described as solitude and society, thought and action, power and form, reason and understanding. They essentially represent the two axes of life, namely, the vertical dimension and the horizontal dimension.

As much as Emerson admired the mystics and visionaries, he thought that success in life had to do with "the skill with which we keep to the diagonal line" between these two axes, as he puts it in "Society and Solitude." In another image, found in "Fate," he insists that we "must ride alternatively on the horses of [our] private and [our] public nature, as the equestrians in the circus throw themselves nimbly from horse to horse, or plant one foot on the back of one, and the other foot on the back of the other."

Undulation, which "shows itself in the inspiring and expiring of the breath," was, for Emerson, another word for polarity, suggesting that the proper course is one that alternates between the two poles of our existence. As he explained in his journal:

> Solitude is naught and society is naught. Alternate them and the good of each is seen. You can soon learn all that society can teach you for one while. . . . Then retire and hide; and from the valley behold the mountain. Have solitary prayer and praise. Love the garden, the barn, the pasture, and the rock. There digest and correct the past experience, blend it with the new and divine life, and grow with God. After some interval when these delights have been sucked dry, accept again the opportunities of society. The same scenes revisited shall wear a new face, shall yield a higher culture. And so on. Undulation, Alternation, is the condition of progress, of life.

Undulation is well and good, but if balance is the goal, it must be the balance of two healthy forces. The problem is that the two poles or forces are not equally well developed in us. The world lacks unity, or balance, because the vertical dimension is atrophied or missing most of the time. Emerson's program for enhancing the spiritual dimension of life and achieving a proper balance between the two modes of consciousness had to do with what he termed "self-culture." The notion itself had antecedents in New England Unitarianism. Emerson applied it to Transcendentalist spirituality.

Though the term might suggest to us something like attending a concert series, a book-discussion group, or an adult-education class, we must remember that, for Emerson, self meant soul. Culture in pre-industrial New England had agrarian connotations. Thus, self-culture is best understood as the cultivation or nurture of the soul. Emerson realized that experiences of insight and ecstasy could not be summoned at will; they required humility, receptiveness, acceptance, and a letting-go of the analytical frame of mind. Even so, such experiences come of their own accord.

Self-culture is a general term applied to several important tasks relating to the spiritual life. The first of these is to heighten awareness through following a course of spiritual discipline or practice. The second is to nurture spiritual growth by cultivating the religious or moral sentiment, that is to say, by growing the soul. The third task is to integrate our spiritual and material lives either by discerning the miraculous in the common or gilding everyday life with the gold-leaf of reality. The fourth is to achieve a certain kind of wisdom gained from experience and reflection. The fifth task is to put these insights and the wisdom gained from them into practice in one's personal, social, and political life. In short, self-culture offered a philosophy and a way of life devoted to achieving and sustaining and living out the consequences of mystical experience, such that "the moments will characterize the days."

In his sermons while he was a minister and in his earliest lectures as a public speaker, Emerson advocated self-culture. In his early lecture "Human Culture," Emerson states, "His own Culture,—the unfolding of his nature, is the chief end of man. A divine impulse at the core of his being impels him to this." He also set down some rules for spiritual practice. One of these was to keep a journal, not so much for what's recorded, "but for the habit of rendering an account of yourself to yourself in some more rigorous manner and at more certain intervals than mere contemplation or casual reverie of solitude require." Another was to cultivate "the simple habit of sitting alone occasionally," to practice contemplation, so that one "may become aware that there around him roll new at this moment and inexhaustible the waters of Life; that the world he has lived in so heedless, so gross, is illuminated with meaning, that every fact is magical; every atom alive, and he is heir of it all." For Emerson, solitude was a necessary condition of the spiritual life.

A third rule was to cultivate an appreciation of nature. "We need nature," Emerson insists in "Human Culture," "and cities give the human senses not room enough. The habit of feeding the senses daily and nightly with the open air and firmament, presently becomes so strong that we feel the want of it like water for washing." Emerson's preferred means of appreciating nature was walking, which he describes in a passage from his journal:

> I do not count the hours I spend in the woods, though I forget my affairs there and my books. And, when there, I wander hither and thither; any bird, any plant, any spring detains me. I do not hurry homewards, for I think all affairs may be postponed to this walking, and it is for this idleness that all my businesses exist.

For a learned and well-read person such as Emerson, it's not surprising that books would provide another means of self-culture. However, he thought that they should be read not for information, but for inspiration. He claimed that he read for what he termed "lustres." Moreover, even for the scholar, he thought books were for idle times: "When he can read God directly, the hour is too precious to be wasted in other men's transcripts of their readings," Emerson writes in "The American Scholar." "But when the intervals of darkness come, as come they must,—when the sun is hid, and the stars withdraw their shining,—we repair to the lamps which were kindled by their ray, to guide our steps to the East again, where the dawn is."

Though not a regular churchgoer, Emerson considered the Sabbath to be an important element of spiritual practice. "I love Sunday Morning," he notes in his journal. "I hail it from afar. I awake with gladness and a holiday feeling always on that day. The Church is ever my desk. If I did not go thither I would not write so many of these wayward pages." As late as 1879, in his lecture "The Preacher," he was extolling the virtues of the Sabbath: "We want some intercalated days, to bethink us and to derive order to our life from the heart. That should be the use of the Sabbath,—to check this headlong racing and put us in possession of ourselves once more."

Emerson especially prized "conversation" as a means of self-culture. He was a member of numerous groups—including the famed Transcendental Club—organized essentially for the purpose of discussing "high questions." The value of conversation as a spiritual practice is described in "The Over-Soul":

> And so in groups where debate is earnest, and especially on high questions, the company become aware that the thought rises to an equal level in all bosoms, that all have a spiritual property in what was said, as well as the sayer. They all become wiser than they were. It arches over them like a temple, this unity of thought, in which every heart beats with nobler sense of power and duty, and thinks and acts with unusual solemnity. All are conscious of attaining to a higher self-possession.

Emerson advocated a combination of "plain living and high thinking" as an antidote to the materialism and shallowness of American society. The practices of contemplation, conversation, reading, and journal writing were intended to cultivate "high thinking." "Plain living" had to do with achieving simplicity and eliminating distractions, cultivating, as it were, a genteel poverty. It was a kind of self-reformation, described in "Man the Reformer" in the following way:

> Can anything be so elegant as to have few wants and to serve them one's self, so as to have somewhat left to give, instead of always being prompt to grab? It is more elegant to answer one's needs, than to be richly served; inelegant perhaps it may look to-day, and to a few, but it is an elegance forever and to all."

As he grew older, Emerson understandably added health and rest to his list of means for the promotion of self-culture. The aim of all of these practices was to cultivate awareness, to nurture spirituality, and to achieve wisdom and balance in life. This aim remained the same for Emerson throughout his life, even though the emphasis shifted with age. With age we encounter yet another paradox of the spiritual life, as indicated in this passage from "Success," one of his later essays:

> We remember when in early youth the earth spoke and the heavens glowed; when an evening, any evening, grim and wintry, sleet and snow, was enough for us; the houses were in the air. Now it costs a rare combination of clouds and lights to overcome the common and mean.

Like most people, Emerson found that the passions of youth diminish with age. Ecstatic experiences of illumination and insight—never numerous to begin with—come with less frequency and intensity as one gets older. His approach to the spiritual life shifted from seeking to recapture such experiences to living life according to the wisdom derived from them. In time the words *undulation* and *alternation* gave way to *continuity* and *consecutiveness*. Unlike his friend Thoreau, who died at the age of forty-four, Emerson lived a long life, in the course of which he traced the trajectory of the soul from youth to old age.

Even as early as 1841, in his lecture "The Transcendentalist," Emerson says (speaking for his imaginary spiritual seeker), "I wish to exchange this flash-of-lightening faith for continuous daylight, this fever glow for a benign climate." In subsequent writings such as "Experience," he suggests that happiness is "to fill the hour and leave no crevice for a repentance or an approval." With a spiritual maturity tempered by the loss of several of those most dear to him, we observe in Emerson a wisdom rooted in an appreciation of the here and now. In "Experience," he writes,

> To finish the moment, to find the journey's end in every step of the road, to live the greatest number of good hours, is wisdom. It is not the part of men, but of fanatics, or of mathematicians, if you will, to say, that, the shortness of life considered, it is not worth caring whether for so short a duration we were sprawling in want, or sitting high. Since our office is with moments, let us husband them. Five minutes of today are worth as much to me, as five minutes in the next millennium. Let us be poised, and wise, and our own, today. . . . Without any shadow of doubt, amidst this vertigo of shows and pol-

itics, I settle myself ever the firmer in the creed, that we should not postpone and refer and wish, but do broad justice where we are, by whomsoever we deal with, accepting our actual companions and circumstances, however humble or odious, as the mystic officials to whom the universe has delegated its whole pleasure for us.

He relishes "the pot-luck of the day" and is "thankful for small mercies." He tells us in "Experience," "If we will take the good we find, asking no questions, we will have heaping measures." He insists,

> The middle region of our being is the temperate zone. We may climb into the thin and cold realm of pure geometry and lifeless science, or sink into that of sensation. Between these extremes is the equator of life, of thought, of spirit, of poetry,—a narrow belt. Moreover, in popular experience, everything good is on the highway.

The goal of the spiritual life is to enrich everyday life with the wisdom of experience. "The luxury of ice is in tropical countries, and midsummer days," Emerson observes in "Power." "The luxury of fire is, to have a little on our hearth: and of electricity, not volleys of the charged cloud, but the manageable stream on the battery wires. So of spirit, or energy. . . ." A steady, continuous flow is advised. Wisdom consists of embracing the here and now, discerning the sublime in the common, and living a committed, moral life.

With advancing years, the days become more precious. In "Works and Days," one of his summary essays from *Solitude and Society*, published in 1870, Emerson writes: "He only is rich who owns the day. There is no king, rich man, fairy or demon who possesses such power as that." The days come and go, he says, "like muffled and veiled figures, sent from a distant friendly party; but they say nothing, and if we do not use the gifts they bring, they carry them as silently away." The challenge is to savor the moment, to appreciate the gifts, however modest, that each day brings:

> The days are made on a loom whereof the warp and woof are past and future time. They are majestically dressed, as if every god brought a thread to the skyey web. 'T is pitiful the things by which we are rich or poor,—a matter of coins, coats and carpets, a little more or less stone, or wood, or paint, the fashion of a cloak or hat. . . . But

the treasures which Nature spent itself to amass,— ... these, not like a glass bead, or the coins or carpets, are given immeasurably to all.

The illusions of daily life deceive and distract us. We think we have time to spare, but we don't. Every day is precious because it's only in the present moment, in this and not some other hour, that life is lived. One of the illusions we entertain is that "the present hour is not the critical decisive hour." Not so, Emerson says in "Works and Days": "Write it on your heart, that every day is the best day of the year. No man has learned anything rightly until he knows that every day is Doomsday."

Another illusion is that there's never enough time for our work. Emerson tells an anecdote in which someone remarks to a certain Native American chief that he doesn't have enough time. The chief replies, "Well, I suppose you have all there is." We always have all the time there is. It's up to us to make the best use of it. It's also an illusion to think that the longer the duration of time—a year, a decade, a century—the better. But "God works in moments," Emerson insists, "We ask for long life, but 'tis deep life, or grand moments that signify." The measure of time should be qualitative, not quantitative. "Moments of insight, of fine personal relation, a smile, a glance,— what ample borrowers of eternity they are!" Eternity culminates in the present moment.

The measure of wisdom is the appreciation of the day. The learned scholar is not one who unearths ancient history, Emerson explains, but rather he who "can unfold the theory of this particular Wednesday." The minutes we are given are not steppingstones to future happiness; in fact, they constitute happiness and the only eternity that exists for us. We must forego our tendency to analyze and dissect experience. Emerson makes this point in the following way:

> ... life is good only when it is magical and musical, a perfect timing and consent, and when we do not anatomize it. You must treat the days respectfully, you must be a day yourself, and not interrogate it like a college professor. The world is enigmatical ... and must not be taken literally, but genially. We must be at the top of our condition to understand anything rightly. You must hear the bird's song without

attempting to render it into nouns and verbs. Cannot we be a little abstemious and obedient? Cannot we let the morning be?

Emerson cites the example of the native Hawaiians, who "delight to play with the surf, coming in on top of the rollers, then swimming out again, and repeat the delicious manoeuvre for hours." The whole of life should be lived in a similar way. Emerson observes that "human life is made up of such transits. . . . There can be no greatness without abandonment. . . . Just to fill the hour,—that is happiness. Fill my hour, ye gods, so that I shall not say, whilst I have done this, 'Behold, also, an hour of my life is gone,'—but rather, 'I have lived an hour.'"

It's the quality of life and not its duration that counts. "It is the depth at which we live," Emerson insists, "and not at all the surface extension that imports." Time is but the flitting surface; with "the least acceleration of thought," we pierce through it to eternity and "make life to seem to be of vast duration." We call it time, but when it's thus penetrated, "it acquires another and higher name." There are some to whom this comes quite naturally, Emerson believed. For the rest of us, it's a matter of gaining wisdom through the pursuit of self-culture.

Emerson's views evolved with the passage of years. A visionary in his thirties, he went through a period of skepticism and disillusionment as a result of personal loss and national crisis leading up to the Civil War. But with age and experience came the wisdom exhibited in his later works. His life was an illustration of his philosophy. "My philosophy holds to a few laws," he noted in a journal entry from the late 1850s. "Flowing, or transition, or shooting the gulf, the perpetual striving to ascend to a higher platform, the same thing in new and higher form." Emerson underwent what David Robinson describes in *Emerson and the Conduct of Life* as a metamorphosis from "agent of rapture" to "agent of fulfillment." Reading Emerson's journal, it is apparent that he regarded this change as nothing but "the same thing in new and higher form." He never ceased to feel that life was an ecstasy and even as he approached old age could affirm: "Within I do not find wrinkles and used heart, but unspent youth."

transcendentalism

1. any of the various philosophies that propose to discover the nature of reality by investigating the process of thought rather than the objects of sense experiences; the philosophies of <u>kant</u>, <u>Hegel</u>, and <u>Fichte</u>.

2. by extension, the philosophical ideas of Emerson and some other 19th century New Englanders, based on a search for reality through spiritual intuition.

3. popularly, any obscure, visionary or idealistic thought

Meantime, whilst the doors of the temple stand open, night and day, before every man, and the oracles of this truth cease never, it is guarded by one stern condition; this, namely; it is an intuition. It cannot be received at second hand. Truly speaking, it is not instruction, but provocation, that I can receive from another soul. What he announces, I must find true in me, or wholly reject, and on his word, . . . be he who he may, I can accept nothing.

Emerson's celebrated "Divinity School Address" was delivered before the senior class in Divinity College at Harvard in July 1838. The invitation came six years after he had resigned his pulpit at Second Church in Boston, and it prompted his most sustained thinking on the nature of religion and the role of ministry outside of his sermons. His remarks stirred considerable debate and the taking of sides between the Unitarian "orthodox" and the Transcendentalists, with the latter defending Emerson. Even today Emerson's words are provocative and revolutionary. The essential message of the address is that "the religious sentiment" is innate and intuitive in human experience. Ministers make religion vital, not by worshipping Jesus or venerating the Bible, but by leading their parishioners to look

within for revelations of the divine and for guidance in living an ethical life. 10 Comand my h

Emerson's argument proceeds from a description of the beauty
and beneficence of nature. The earth is viewed as a natural communion of corn and wine, an "original blessing," in spiritual theolo-
gian Matthew Fox's use of the term. Emerson is laying the
groundwork for a theology based not on doctrine, scripture, or tradition, but on an understanding and appreciation of the natural
world, which is suffused with "laws which traverse the universe and
make things the way they are." These laws are essentially moral in
nature and awaken in us "the sentiment of virtue." They "refuse to be
adequately stated," says Emerson, and "elude our persevering
thought; yet we read them hourly in each other's faces, in each other's
actions, in our own remorse."

For Emerson, "this sentiment is the essence of all religion." He
goes on to describe the nature of the moral laws that give rise to
it. In the first place, these laws are universal. "They are out of time,
out of space, and not subject to circumstance." Thus in the human
soul "there is a justice whose retributions are instant and entire."
Those who do a good deed are instantly ennobled; those who do
a mean deed are just as surely diminished. If we deceive or dis-
semble, we are alienated from ourselves and out of sync with the
world.

Second, these laws are certain and inexorable. "Character is always
known," Emerson says. "Thefts never enrich; alms never impoverish;
murder will speak out of stone walls." By the same token, "speak the
truth, and all nature and all spirits help you with unexpected fur-
therance. Speak the truth, and all things alive or brute are vouchers,
and the very roots of the grass there do seem to stir and move to bear
you witness." That is to say, if we have integrity—if we are at one with
ourselves—we will also be in harmony with the world. Like attracts
like, whether good or evil.

In the third place, these laws proceed from one will, one mind,
everywhere active, "in each ray of the star, in each wavelet of the
pool," and whatever opposes it is ultimately defeated. Emerson is a
monist, not a dualist. For him, good is positive. Evil is merely "priv-

1. universal
2. certain + inexorable —cannot be removed by
    Persuasion
3 proceed from one will

34

ative," not absolute. It's like cold, which is the absence of heat. "All evil is so much death or nonentity." Benevolence alone is absolute and real:

> All things proceed out of the same spirit, and all things conspire with it. Whilst a man seeks good ends, he is strong by the whole strength of nature. In so far as he roves from these ends, he bereaves himself of power ... his being shrinks ... he becomes less and less, a mote, a point, until absolute badness is absolute death.

The perception of this law awakens the moral sentiment, which is the key to human happiness. "The assurance that Law is sovereign over all of nature" means that we live in a moral universe and therefore have a basis for morality that is independent of doctrine and scripture. Because human beings are part and parcel of the natural world, "the fountain of all good" is equally in us. Each person is "an inlet into the deeps of Reason" and, because of this, intuitively knows right from wrong.

In Emerson's view, "This sentiment lies at the foundation of society, and successively creates all forms of worship." Because it is innate, it never entirely dies out. The purest expressions of this sentiment are sublime and are to be found "not alone in Palestine," but also in Egypt, Persia, India, and China. As Emerson is at pains to show, this sentiment is a direct intuition into the nature of things and can't be had from other persons or past ages. The history of the Christian church reflects this degradation of primary faith. Emerson concedes that Jesus "belonged to the true race of prophets." Alone in history, Jesus recognized the greatness of humanity and the infinite possibilities of human life. "One man was true to what is in you and me. He saw that God incarnates himself in man, and evermore goes forth to take possession of his World." But the Christian church has distorted Jesus' message. Christianity has replaced Jesus the man with Jesus the myth, and "churches are built not on his principles, but his tropes." The miracles ascribed to him are an example of what the church has done. "He spoke of miracles; for he felt that man's life was a miracle," Emerson says. "But the word Miracle, as pronounced by Christian churches, gives a false impression; it is Monster. It is not one with the blowing clover and the falling rain."

Historical Christianity has made the mistake of exaggerating the *person* of Jesus. But, according to Emerson, the soul "knows no persons. It invites every man to expand to the full circle of the universe." Instead of ascribing greatness to humanity, as Jesus did, the churches have reserved it only for Jesus, painting him a demigod and elevating him so much above the rest of us that they have vitiated the power of his example. In effect, what the churches teach is this: "That you shall not own the world; you shall not dare and live after the infinite Law that is in you, . . . but you must subordinate your nature to Christ's nature; you must accept our interpretations, and take his portrait as the vulgar draw it."

To the contrary, Emerson says, "That is always best which gives me to myself. The sublime is excited in me by the stoical doctrine, Obey thyself. That which shows God in me, fortifies me. That which shows God out of me, makes me a wart and a wen." The great religious teachers evoke our own goodness by the power of their example. Jesus serves us likewise, and not by virtue of the miracles he's alleged to have performed. To aim to convert followers by an appeal to miracles is "a profanation of the soul." Not by miracles, but "only by coming again to themselves, or to God in themselves, can [people] grow forevermore."

A second defect of historical Christianity, related to the first, is that the soul is not considered the basis of our moral nature, only a revelation given once and for all long ago. But "the spirit only can teach," Emerson says. Only the one on whom the soul descends and through whom it speaks has authority. Because the church relies instead on scripture and dogma as the basis of authority, it totters on the brink of extinction.

It's incumbent upon ministers to preach the doctrine of the soul. "Preaching," says Emerson, "is the expression of the moral sentiment in application to the duties of life." But the office of preaching is not being discharged:

> In how many churches, by how many prophets, tell me, is man
> made sensible that he is an infinite Soul; that the earth and heavens

are passing into his mind; that he is drinking forever the soul of God?

Instead, many ministers are formalists who preach doctrine rather than faith. "Faith," Emerson insists, "should blend with the light of rising and of setting suns, with the flying cloud, the singing bird, and the breath of flowers. But now the priest's Sabbath has lost the splendor of nature; it is unlovely; we are glad when it is done."

Emerson describes a service he attended in his church in Concord that left him quite disappointed. The minister gave no indication that he had ever laughed or wept, had ever been commended or cheated or chagrined, no indication that he had ever lived at all. "The true preacher," to the contrary, "can be known by this, that he deals out to the people his life,—life passed through the fire of thought." Ministers do not always preach effectively, Emerson says, but woe to those who are "called to the pulpit and *not* give the bread of life." Too much preaching "comes out of the memory, and not out of the soul." It is traditional and routine and turns people away from the churches.

The loss of worship leads to the decay of society. What can be done to change this situation? The inertness of religion, which results from closing the book on revelation and worshipping Jesus instead of presenting him as a man, indicates the error of our ways:

> It is the office of a true teacher to show us that God is, not was; that He speaketh, not spake. The true Christianity,—a faith like Christ's in the infinitude of man—is lost. None believeth in the soul of man, but only in some man or person old and departed.

Secondary knowledge is insufficient. Emerson admonishes the students to go alone, "to love God without mediator or veil." Forego imitation and stultifying habit: "Yourself a newborn bard of the Holy Ghost, cast behind you all conformity, and acquaint man at first hand with Deity."

For all our slavery to routine and "penny-wisdom," we do have sublime thoughts and value the few times when we feel awake and alive. We also remember times when ministers made our souls wiser, when they spoke what we thought, told us what we knew, and encouraged us to be what we inwardly are. The remedy to a lifeless formalism in the pulpit is "first soul, and second, soul, and evermore, soul." Christianity has given us the Sabbath, Emerson insists, and the institution of preaching. Ministers should breath new life into these forms and demonstrate that the "supreme Beauty which ravished the souls of those Eastern men . . . and through their lips spoke oracles to all time, shall speak in the West also."

Emerson's "Divinity School Address" was a watershed document in American religious history and in the evolution of Unitarianism. Unitarians in Emerson's day were more liberal in their views than other Christians, but tended to believe that Jesus was divine, even if he was not God. They believed in the Christian revelation and the historical validity of the Gospels and, as evidence, insisted on the veracity of the miracles performed by Jesus. They believed in the transcendence and the personality of God, and they believed that morality was grounded in scripture and doctrine, assisted by the use of reason.

Emerson's address flew in the face of these views. In the course of his remarks, he denied the personality and transcendence of God, asserting instead that God was an impersonal law or soul immanent in the world. In this he was accused, with some justification, of pantheism. He insisted that Jesus was a human being who realized the potential to identify with God and, in providing a model, made that a possibility for others as well. Every person, in Emerson's way of thinking, "may expand to the full circle of the universe." In denying the divinity of Jesus, he rejected the validity of the miracles as well. In place of scripture and doctrine as the basis of morality, he grounded goodness in an intuition of the moral laws that suffuse the universe.

Since, for Emerson, God is within the human soul, religion is universal and immediate. Religion is not based on a particular revelation that occurred once and for all long ago. Nor is it a hand-me-down sort of thing, dependent for its existence and validity on scripture, doctrine, or ecclesiastical authority. Religion is a present reality, grounded in nature and human experience, or it is nothing. It's the minister's role and duty to preach "the doctrine of the soul," namely, to make man "sensible that he is an infinite Soul; that the earth and the heavens are passing into his mind; that he is drinking forever the soul of God."

⑥

Creation is original blessing, and all the subsequent blessings—those we give our loved ones and those we struggle to bring about by healing, celebration, and justice making—are prefigured in the original blessing that creation is, a blessing so thoroughly unconditional, so fully graced, that we can go through life hardly noticing it at all. Our religions are capable of building their magnificent temples, housing their vast followers, teaching their elaborate catechisms, and raising their considerable sums of money, but forgetting entirely about the grace of creation. Boredom, depression, and what our ancestors called the sin of "acedia" (or ennui) occur when we get cut off from the sense of grace and blessing.

—Matthew Fox, *Creation Spirituality*

In one sense at least the personal religion will prove itself more fundamental than either theology or ecclesiasticism. Churches, when once established, live at second-hand upon their tradition; but the founders of every church owed their power originally to the fact of their direct personal communion with the divine. Not only the superhuman founders, the Christ, the Buddha, Mahomet, but all the originators of Christian sects have been in this case;—so personal religion should still seem the primordial thing, even to those who continue to esteem it incomplete.

—William James, *The Varieties of Religious Experience*

Questions for Personal Reflection and Group Discussion

- Emerson begins the Divinity School Address with a meditation on what Matthew Fox might term "original blessing," an appeal for an earth-based spirituality. Why do you suppose he does this?

- Emerson aimed to ground morality in nature and human nature. He believed that "the sentiment of virtue" is innate in human experience and that the natural world is suffused with "laws which traverse the universe and make things the way they are." Do you agree? What is the ground of your moral sensibility, your sense of right and wrong?

- Emerson rejected scripture and doctrine as the basis of faith, insisting that religion "cannot be received at second hand." For him spirituality is a matter of personal experience. What is the basis of faith for you?

- Emerson denied the divinity of Jesus, the veracity of miracles, and the personality of God. On the other hand, he believed very strongly in what he termed "the infinitude of man." What are your views on Jesus, miracles, God, and man? Do you find yourself in agreement with Emerson?

- "In how many churches," Emerson asks, "is man made sensible that he is an infinite Soul; that the earth and heavens are passing into his mind; that he is drinking forever the soul of God?" Is this true of your experience of church? Do you think it should be?

- For all of his criticism of religious institutions, Emerson felt that we should not abandon them, but breathe new life into them. What's your view? Can religion, as we understand the word today, be saved?

- Some argue that Emerson's (and William James's) stress on personal experience has the effect of encouraging individualism at the expense of religious institutions. Do you agree?

SELF-RELIANCE

We lie in the lap of immense intelligence, which makes us receivers of its truth and organs of its activity. When we discern justice, when we discern truth, we do nothing of ourselves, but allow a passage to its beams. If we ask whence this comes, if we seek to pry into the soul that causes, all philosophy is at fault. Its presence or its absence is all we can affirm. Every man discriminates between the voluntary acts of his mind, and his involuntary perceptions, and knows that to his involuntary perceptions a perfect faith is due. He may err in the expression of them, but he knows that these things are so, like day and night, not to be disputed.

"Self-Reliance" originally appeared in Emerson's first series of essays, published in 1841 at the height of his powers as a writer and thinker. The essay is a celebration of genius, which Emerson and the Transcendentalists valued very highly. But the word *genius* meant something different for them. For us the word connotes great intelligence or talent; for the Transcendentalists it meant something more like a current of energy or power that can be tapped. In their view, virtually any person could demonstrate genius if he allowed this current to flow through him in an unobstructed way. It could be said that the essay represents a demonstration of Emerson's own genius, an assertion of his strongly held conviction that each of us should find and pursue the mission in life that's uniquely ours to fulfill.

Unfortunately, the essay is frequently misunderstood to commend an unbridled individualism. But the self that Emerson refers to is not the ego or the isolated self of modern philosophy or psychology. It's the soul, which, though uniquely incarnated in each individual, is nevertheless commonly shared by everything that exists as an expression of what, in another well-known essay, Emerson calls the oversoul. Thus, self-reliance is not reliance on the self in isolation, but on the self in relation to the larger self that "makes us receivers of its truth and organs of its activity."

Perhaps this helps us to understand what Emerson says in the opening paragraph of the most famous of his essays:

> To believe your own thought, to believe that what is true for you in your private heart is true for all men,—that is genius. Speak your latent conviction, and it shall be the universal sense; for the inmost in due time becomes the outmost,—and our first thought is rendered back to us by the trumpets of the Last Judgment.

In a paradoxical way, the thoughts that are unique to us are apt to be universal as well, since they represent the universal mind speaking through us. Moses, Plato, and Milton are considered geniuses because they said what they were inspired to say, not what others thought. Unfortunately, we tend to reject our own thoughts only to hear them in the words of another.

"Imitation is suicide," Emerson declares. We must till the soil that is given to us alone. "The power which resides" in each of us "is new in nature" and no one but us knows what we can do until we've tried. The failure to assert ourselves renders us impotent. "Trust thyself: every heart vibrates to that iron string." The young are naturally self-reliant by insisting on themselves. But as we grow up, there's increasing pressure to conform.

Society conspires against uniqueness and originality, prompting Emerson to proclaim that "whoso would be a man must be a nonconformist. . . . Nothing is at last sacred but the integrity of your own mind." There are those who consider self-reliance too subjective as the basis of authority, but as Emerson says, "no law can be sacred to me but that of my nature." For good or ill, we have only ourselves to go by, our own sense of right and wrong.

People tend to defer to the authority of others. Instead, they should speak the truth as they see it, even if it seems a little rude. Goodness, after all, "must have some edge to it." And we must be prepared to "shun father and mother and wife and brother" when genius calls, though it appear like "whim" to others. There's no goodness by proxy or out of a sense of duty. We must do what we are motivated to do, not what others think we should do. "It is easy," Emerson says, "to live after the world's opinion; it is easy in solitude to live after our own." What's difficult is to keep the independence of solitude in the midst of the crowd.

The problem with conformity is that "it scatters your force." One becomes a cipher rather than an individual. We are known by what we do. If we conform, we are predictable, false, and partial persons. Still, the pressures to conform are great, and for failure to do so, "the world whips you with its displeasure."

The desire for consistency also undermines our self-trust. We shouldn't be afraid to question past judgments, even if it seems that we contradict ourselves. So what, Emerson seems to say:

> A foolish consistency is the hobgoblin of little minds, adored by little statesmen and philosophers and divines. With consistency a great soul has simply nothing to do. . . . Speak what you think now in hard words and to-morrow speaks what to-morrow thinks in hard words again, though it contradict everything you said to-day.

It's better to be misunderstood than to not speak the truth that is given us today. All great minds were misunderstood.

If we're honest with ourselves, our integrity or symmetry will be apparent in every instance. In the end "we pass for what we are," Emerson says. "Character teaches above our wills. Men imagine that they communicate their virtue or vice only by overt action, and not see that virtue or vice emit a breath every instant." Actions that are honest and natural will also be harmonious. Each one reveals who you are in a way that conformity and consistency alone can never do.

Great people are those who have the courage to be themselves. Each one is "a cause, a country, and an age." And others follow their lead. "An institution is the lengthened shadow of one man." Therefore, we must be our own persons and not mendicants or sycophants. Why this deference to others, Emerson wonders.

The impulse toward original action is explained by the nature of self-trust. "Who is the Trustee?" Emerson asks. "What is the aboriginal Self, on which a universal reliance can be grounded?" Self-reliance is reliance on spontaneity or instinct. "We denote this primary wisdom as Intuition, whilst all later teachings are tuitions." Intuition of the supreme mind is the end goal of truth for us. Behind this we cannot go. There's a oneness of things that we discern intuitively "in calm hours," a oneness that includes us and proceeds from the same source that we do. This source is the fountain of all action and thought, "the lungs of that inspiration which giveth man wisdom and cannot be denied without impiety and atheism."

In the passage that begins this chapter, Emerson elaborates on an essentially mystical way of knowing: What's needed to apprehend the truth of this proposition is an uncluttered, attentive mind. And when the mind receives this divine wisdom, "old things pass away,— means, teachers, texts, temples fall; it lives now, and absorbs past and future in the present hour." All things are here and now. Those who speak of a revelation that is rooted in the past are false to this truth. Rather than saying what we think, we quote "some saint or sage." But all things exist in the eternal now: "These roses under my window make no reference to former roses or to better ones; they are for what they are; they exist with God to-day. There is no time to them. There is simply the rose; it is perfect in every moment of its existence." We do not live in the present ourselves, but, "with reverted eye," lament the past or, heedless of the riches that surround us, stand "on tiptoe to foresee the future." We will never be "happy and strong" until we too live "with nature in the present, above time."

We find it hard to believe the truth of Emerson's remarks unless it's expressed in the words of "David, or Jeremiah, or Paul." "We are like children who repeat by rote the sentences of grandames and tutors." When we have our own perceptions, "we shall gladly disburden the memory of its hoarded treasures as old rubbish." The truth he speaks of can't be known in any accustomed way; "you cannot discern the footprints of any other." It goes out from us, not in to us. In Emerson's view, the truth of the matter is this:

> Life only avails, not the having lived. Power ceases in the moment of repose; it resides in the moment of transition from a past to a new state, in the shooting of the gulf, in the darting to an aim. This one fact the world hates; that the soul *becomes*; for that forever degrades the past, turns all riches to poverty, all reputation to a shame, confounds the saint with the rogue, shoves Jesus and Judas equally aside. Why then do we prate of self-reliance? Inasmuch as the soul is present there will be power not confident but agent. To talk of reliance is a poor external way of speaking. Speak rather of that which relies because it works and is.

Self-reliance is reliance on "the ever-blessed One," the supreme cause. All things are real by virtue of the fact that they are penetrated by this oneness. And because the soul is thus self-sufficing, it may also be self-relying. "God," Emerson says, "is within." Instead of putting ourselves "in communication with the internal ocean," we go "abroad to beg a cup of water of the urns of other men."

"We must go alone," Emerson insists, even if it means a break from our accustomed ways. If we don't follow the dictates of our own nature, we risk being hypocrites. Others will say that rejecting popular standards means breaking with all standards and that "the bold sensualist will use the name of philosophy to gild his crimes." But a code higher than the popular one makes its own stern claims. "If any one imagines that this law is lax, let him keep its commandment one day."

The present state of society suggests that people are afraid to assert themselves. They "are afraid of truth, afraid of fortune, afraid of death, afraid of each other." Society needs self-reliant persons, but most people are "insolvent" and "cannot satisfy their own wants." Our arts, occupations, marriages, and religion are chosen for us, not by us. A greater self-reliance would effect a revolution in our thoughts, our relationships, and our modes of living.

Emerson's gospel of self-reliance informs his thinking about four topics in particular, the first of which is prayer. Prayer, for Emerson, "is the contemplation of the facts of life from the highest point of view." He rejects petitionary prayer as "meanness and theft." If we are one with God, he says, we will not beg. There is, in fact, "prayer in all action," as in the Buddhist notion of *darshan*, or work as a form of contemplation. Our regrets are also false prayers, inasmuch as they represent a failure of self-reliance. As most prayers represent "a disease of the will," so our creeds are "a disease of the intellect." Instead of thinking for ourselves, we let others do our thinking for us.

For one who seems to have benefited from his own travels, Emerson nevertheless insists that "the soul is no traveller." He means that the soul is—or should be—at home wherever it goes. If we travel for amusement or distraction, we merely bring our problems and preoccupations along with us, carrying "ruins to ruins," as Emerson says.

The intellect is also a vagabond, and we end up following the paths of other minds rather than forging ahead our own. "Insist on yourself," Emerson admonishes us, "never imitate. Your own gift you can present every moment with the cumulative force of a whole life's cultivation; but of the adopted talent of another you have only an extemporaneous half-possession." Every great person is unique and not a copy of someone else. "The Scipionism of Scipio is precisely that part he could not borrow. Shakespeare will never be made by the study of Shakespeare."

Society appears to progress, but it recedes as fast as it gains. Our so-called improvements do us little good. "A civilized man has built a coach, but has lost the use of his feet." In our "refinements" we lose our energy or force, "the vigor of wild virtue." Humanity has not progressed over time, though the discoveries of science and exploration may make it appear so. It advances only to the extent that people learn to be self-reliant, to measure the worth of each other by what each is, not what each has. Our fortunes may rise or fall. Things may go our way, and we think good days are finally here. But do not believe it. "Nothing can give you peace but yourself. Nothing can bring you peace but the triumph of principles."

＠

We arrive in this world with birthright gifts—then we spend the first half of our lives abandoning them or letting others disabuse us of them. As young people, we are surrounded by expectations that may have little to do with who we really are, expectations held by people who are not trying to discern our selfhood but to fit us into slots. In families, schools, workplaces, and religious communities, we are trained away from true self toward images of acceptability; under social pressures like racism and sexism our original shape is deformed beyond recognition; and we ourselves, driven by fear, too often betray true self to gain the approval of others.

We are disabused of original giftedness in the first half of our lives. Then—if we are awake, aware, and able to admit our loss—we spend the second half of life trying to recover and reclaim the gift we once possessed.
—Parker J. Palmer, *Let Your Life Speak*

The authentic self is the you that can be found at your absolute core. It is the part of you that is not defined by your job, or your function, or your role. It is the composite of all your unique gifts, skills, abilities, interests, talents, insights, and wisdom. It is all of your strengths and values that are uniquely yours and need expression, versus what you have been programmed to believe that you are "supposed" to be and do. It is the you that flourished, unself-consciously, in those times of your life when you felt happiest and most fulfilled. It is the you that existed before and remains when life's pain, experiences, and expectancies are stripped away.
—Philip C. McGraw, *Self Matters*

Questions for Personal Reflection and Group Discussion

- To what extent and in which respects do you feel the need to conform to the expectations of others?

- Do you agree with Emerson, Palmer, and McGraw that society conspires against uniqueness and individuality?

- Have you ever done anything on a whim because it felt like the right thing to do at the time?

- Do you agree that "a foolish consistency is the hobgoblin of little minds"? Or do you think it's a virtue to always be consistent?

- Have you ever done something because you felt that you were somehow meant to do it? Would you say you were responding to your genius?

- Are people generally reluctant or afraid to assert themselves? Have you ever failed to assert yourself and later wished that you had done so?

- What is your unique gift, without which the world would be the lesser for?

- Emerson suggests that we shouldn't fear the displeasure of others or be afraid that our actions might be disruptive. Goodness, he says, should have some edge to it and that in conformity we lose "the vigor of wild virtue." Does this make sense to you? Do you agree?

COMPENSATION

Thus is the universe alive. All things are moral. That soul which within us is a sentiment, outside of us is a law. . . . Justice is not postponed. A perfect equity adjusts its balance in all parts of life. . . . The dice of God are always loaded. The world looks like a multiplication-table, or a mathematical equation, which, turn it how you will, balances itself. . . . Every secret is told, every crime is punished, every virtue rewarded, every wrong redressed, in silence and certainty. What we call retribution is the universal necessity by which the whole appears wherever a part appears.

"Compensation," published in 1841 in Emerson's first series of essays, is one of the most difficult to discuss for the very reason Emerson himself alludes to in the opening paragraph, namely, the discrepancy that exists between life and theology. By this he means our experience of life as opposed to our interpretations of it, especially when these interpretations are based on religious dogma and doctrine. In Emerson's view, compensation, as he understands the word, is validated intuitively even if it's misunderstood intellectually. The notion of compensation enjoys considerable currency in some circles even today.

The insight on which Emerson's argument is based was, by his own account, one that he had as a young boy and continued to intrigue him as an adult. He was apparently inspired to write the essay when he heard a preacher argue that "judgment is not executed in this world; that the wicked are successful; that the good are miserable." The preacher then urged "from reason and from Scripture a compensation to be made to both parties in the next life." Emerson takes issue with this doctrine and with the assumptions that the wicked prosper and that justice is done in the next world, but not in this one.

Our daily experience gives this doctrine the lie. People "are wiser than they know," even when they can't demonstrate the falsehood of a particular proposition. It's Emerson's intention here to make the case, as best he can, for an opposing point of view. The law of compensation is rooted in the principle of polarity, which is established in nature:

> Polarity, or action and reaction, we meet in every part of nature; in darkness and light; in heat and cold; in the ebb and flow of waters; in male and female; in the inspiration and expiration of plants and animals; in the equation of quality and quantity in the fluids of the animal body; in the systole and diastole of the heart; in the undulations of fluids and of sound; in the centrifugal and centripetal gravity; in electricity, galvanism, and chemical affinity.

This dualism is found everywhere in nature, suggesting that each thing is a half that requires its complement to make it a whole, such as spirit and matter, man and woman, odd and even, over and under, motion and rest, and so forth. Nature doesn't favor one of these poles over another, "but a certain compensation balances every gift and every defect." This is true of mechanical forces as well as living creatures.

Emerson insists that the same dualism underlies the human condition, such that for every gain there's a loss, for every evil, a good. A leveling tendency in the natural order of things "puts down the overbearing, the strong, the rich, the fortunate, substantially on the same ground with all others." There's a price to pay for everything. "The President has paid dear for his White House." His power and position have cost him his peace of mind. The law of compensation applies not only to individuals, but to cities and nations as well. Though we may conspire against it, the law will eventually assert itself. A system of moral checks and balances prevails.

If this is so, it's because "the universe is represented in every one of its particles. Everything in nature contains all the powers of nature. Every thing is made of one hidden stuff. . . ." As all things are related by virtue of their common nature, so also is every occupation, art, and human transaction "a compend of the world and a correlative of every other. Each one is an entire emblem of human life; of its good and ill, its trials, its enemies, its course and its end."

"The world globes itself in a drop of dew," Emerson observes. The microcosm is a reflection of the macrocosm. "The true doctrine of omnipresence is that God reappears with all his parts in every moss and cobweb." Therefore all things are moral. Justice is inescapable. "Every secret is told," says Emerson, "every crime is punished, every virtue rewarded, every wrong redressed, in silence and certainty. What we call retribution is the universal necessity by which the whole appears everywhere a part appears." There are two kinds of retribution, the one affecting the inner nature, the other affecting the outward appearance. What we tend to look for in the way of retribution is some outward manifestation of punishment or reward, which may take time to be revealed. But retribution affecting the inner nature actually accompanies the offense.

Unfortunately, we live our lives in a piecemeal fashion. The world wants to be taken as a whole, but we "seek to act partially, to sunder, to appropriate." We aim to possess only the sweet side of nature, without the bitter part. Nature will not have it so. "We can no more halve things and get the sensual good, by itself, than we can get an inside that shall have no outside, or a light without a shadow." We try to escape the inevitable conditions of our existence, but they are in our very soul and can't be evaded. "So signal is the failure of all attempts to make this separation of the good from the tax, that the experiment would not be tried,—since to try it is mad. . . ."

Once we're infected with the desire to separate, we cease "to see God whole in every object." We see "the mermaid's head but not the dragon's tail," and we think we can sever the part we want from the part we don't. There is, in fact, "a crack in every thing God has made," such that human beings only think they can shake themselves "free of the old laws." Always there is "this back-stroke, this kick of the gun, certifying that the law is fatal; that in nature nothing can be given, all things are sold."

The myths and fables and proverbs of all cultures affirm the folly of trying to pick and choose. These represent intuitions into the law of laws, "which the pulpit, the senate and the college deny." The truth of the matter is that "all things are double, one against another," affirmed in sayings so universal as to be commonplace: tit for tat, measure for measure, give and it shall be given to you. For every action there will be a reaction that is inherent in the action itself. This is true of human behavior also. Every word we utter is a judgment upon ourselves. One "cannot do wrong without suffering wrong." Those who try to exclude others close the door on themselves.

Fear is the punishment for all infractions of love and equity in our social relations. Oppression creates hatred in the oppressed and fear in the oppressor. "Fear is an instructor of great sagacity," Emerson observes, "and the herald of all revolutions." Where there's fear, there are invariably "great wrongs which must be revised." Our debts of service to others are best paid off as we go along. Otherwise resentments creep into the relationship, and what had been a transaction between equals becomes an exchange between one who is superior and another who is inferior. This is true of all transactions, not just those between individuals. "Always pay," Emerson insists, "for first or last you must pay your entire debt." It can't be postponed for long.

> Benefit is the end of nature. But for every benefit which you receive, a tax is levied. He is great who confers the most benefits. He is base,— and that is the one base thing in the universe,—to receive favors and render none. In the order of nature we cannot render benefits to those from whom we receive them, or only seldom. But the benefit we received must be rendered again, line for line, deed for deed, cent for cent, to somebody. Beware of too much good staying in your hand. It will fast corrupt and worm worms. Pay it away quickly in some sort.

There can be no cheating or theft because there can be no gain from these. Things may be taken or counterfeited, but what they represent—virtue and knowledge—cannot be. "The law of nature is, Do the thing, and you shall have the power; but they who do not the thing have not the power." As with the Hindu doctrine of *karma*, there's an "absolute balance of Give and Take" in Emerson's view of the universe:

> ... the doctrine that everything has its price,—and if that price is not paid, not that thing but something else is obtained, and that it is impossible to get anything without its price,—is not less sublime in the columns of a ledger than in the budgets of states, in the laws of light and darkness, in all the action and reaction of nature.

Therefore do nature and virtue offer a united front to vice. "Commit a crime, and the earth is made of glass."

On the other hand, nature and virtue conspire to reward all right action. "Love and you shall be loved." The virtuous are befriended even by their faults, and their strength grows out of their weakness. While we sit on the cushion of our advantages, we go to sleep. But when we're "pushed, tormented, defeated," we have a chance to learn something. We've been put on our wits and cured of "the insanity of conceit." It's better to be blamed than to be praised, for "every evil to which we do not succumb is a benefactor" and "we gain the strength of the temptation we resist."

We are wrong to think that we can be cheated. We can only cheat ourselves. "There is a third silent party to all our bargains," in Emerson's view. "The nature and soul of things takes on itself the guaranty of the fulfillment of every contract, so that honest service cannot come to loss." Those who persecute others will find that their efforts cannot succeed. "The martyr cannot be dishonored."

The fact that everything has a positive and a negative side and that "every advantage has its tax" doesn't mean that good and evil cancel each other out; "the doctrine of compensation is not the doctrine of indifferency." Beneath the ebb and flow of life is the soul, which partakes of being itself. "Essence, or God, is not a relation or a part, but the whole. Being is the vast affirmative, excluding negation, self-balanced, and swallowing up all relations, parts and time within itself. Nature, truth, virtue, are the influx from thence. Vice is the absence or departure of the same."

We feel cheated when criminals appear to get away with their crimes. But they haven't outwitted the law of compensation. "Inasmuch as [the criminal] carries the malignity and the lie with him he so far deceases from nature." In some way or other this will be apparent, but there's retribution even when it's not obvious. On the other hand, there's no price to be paid for virtue or wisdom. "There can be no excess to love, none to knowledge, none to beauty, when these attributes are considered in the purest sense. The soul refuses limits, and always affirms an Optimism, never a Pessimism."

External goods have their tax, but not intrinsic ones. Possessions, honors, powers, persons—these come at a price. Wisdom and peace of mind are free for the taking. "In the nature of the soul is the compensation for the inequalities of condition." It seems a great injustice that some have less than others. But no matter how overshadowed and outdone by others, we can still love and still receive. "It is the nature of the soul to appropriate all things." Jesus and Shakespeare are fragments of the soul. Therefore, what they had, we can have also.

Personal calamities, like inequalities of condition, are opportunities for growth. But we must learn to let go. We find it hard to believe that the future could be as beautiful as the remembered past. "We linger in the ruins of an old tent where we once had bread and shelter and organs, nor believe that the spirit can feed, cover and nerve us again. We cannot again find aught so dear, so sweet, so graceful. But we sit and weep in vain. The voice of the Almighty saith, 'Up and onward for evermore!' We cannot stay amid the ruins."

The compensations of calamity are made apparent over time. Our losses seem overwhelming and unredeemable at the time. "But the sure years reveal the deep remedial force that underlies all facts." Speaking from his own painful experience, Emerson assures us that the "death of a dear friend, wife, brother, lover, which seemed nothing but privation, somewhat later assumes the aspect of a guide or genius; for it commonly operates revolutions in our way of life, terminates an epoch of infancy or of youth which was waiting to be closed, breaks up a wonted occupation, or a household, or style of living, and allows the formation of new ones more friendly to the growth of character." Were it not for life's challenges, we might have remained "a sunny garden-flower" with shallow roots and too much sunshine, rather than become a "banian of the forest, yielding shade and fruit to wide neighborhoods" of fellow human beings.

⑥

The idea of Karma is not regarded in India as a theological doctrine or as an intellectual speculation; it is considered to offer the only rational, logical and satisfactory explanation of all the perplexities and problems of human life. The word Karma, from the Sanscrit, literally means "action," that is, all that we think, all that we do, and also whatever is produced as the result of our thought and deed. . . . In India the idea of Karma is not a mere dogmatic belief; it is a fundamental law and corresponds to what modern science calls the law of cause and effect. It shows that there is no such thing as chance or injustice in human affairs; that all these inequalities which we see in the world are not ordained by an arbitrary Ruler, but are the inevitable results of our own mode of life and thought.

—Swami Paramananda, *Emerson and Vedanta*

Thich Nhat Hanh says that "nothing exists by itself alone. Everything has to be with everything else in the cosmos. For example, if you look deeply into a flower you will also see the sun, the clouds, the seeds, the soil. Every flower is made up of these non-flower elements." This is another way to understand karma. Karma says that all actions inter-be with all other actions and therefore all things are part of each other. Everything we do affects everything. Do we want our actions to create peace and love and harmony or do we want them to contribute to more suffering? We have that choice at every moment of our lives.

—Elizabeth Lesser, *The New American Spirituality*

Questions for Personal Reflection and Group Discussion

• How are the wicked of the world held accountable? Is there any accountability if they never get caught?

55

- What, if anything, do the polarities of nature and human experience mean for you?

- Are those who do wrong diminished in some way by their actions?

- Emerson insists that we cannot possess the sweet side of nature without the bitter part. Do you agree?

- What's your opinion concerning the Hindu and Buddhist doctrines of *karma*? Do you agree with the notion yourself?

- Is there any downside to love, beauty, knowledge, virtue, or service to others? Are they always, as Emerson seems to think, positive enlargements of the soul?

- What, if anything, have you learned from the calamities in your life?

- Have you ever experienced a loss that in the end caused a revolution in your outlook on life?

There is a soul at the center of nature and over the will of every man, so that none of us can wrong the universe. It has so infused its strong enchantment into nature that we prosper when we accept its advice, and when we struggle to wound its creatures our hands are glued to our sides. The whole course of things goes to teach us faith. We need only obey. There is a guidance for each of us, and by lowly listening we shall hear the right word. Why need you choose so painfully your place and occupation and associates and modes of action and of entertainment? Certainly there is a possible right for you that precludes the need of balance and willful election. For you there is a reality, a fit place and congenial duties. Place yourself in the middle of the stream of power and wisdom which animates all it floats, and you are without effort impelled to truth, to right and a perfect contentment.

"Spiritual Laws," an essay from the 1841 series, attempts to strike a balance between action and repose. Emerson suggests that repose, or contemplation, is the necessary ground of all meaningful action. Action that is based on social expectations or emulation of others is neither authentic nor worthwhile. Moreover, the will, the ego, and the mind are all impediments to action, which must be natural and unforced to be effective. By contemplation we may discern the natural course of things. Surrendering ourselves to the way of nature, we will discover that our actions gain in power, effectiveness, and integrity.

When we are in a contemplative frame of mind "we discover that our life is embosomed in beauty." The "familiar and stale" as well as the "tragic and terrible" assume a certain grace and comeliness. The soul is untouched by deformity or pain, and we cannot say that we have ever made a sacrifice. At such times we find that "all loss, all pain, is particular; the universe remains to the heart unhurt." It is only the finite that suffers; "the infinite lies stretched in smiling repose."

We may keep our minds clean and healthful if we live the life of nature and don't trouble ourselves with difficulties. Unfortunately, Emerson observes, the young seem to be "diseased with the theological problems of original sin, origin of evil, predestination and the like." But such ideas never trouble anyone who does not go out of his or her way to seek them. "These are the soul's mumps and measles and whooping-coughs," Emerson insists. "A simple mind will not know these enemies."

Spiritual growth is encouraged by allowing for a certain "natural magnetism." If not constrained, the mind "is sure to select what belongs to it." The same is true of our moral nature. We think virtue is a struggle, when, in fact, we would be naturally virtuous if we didn't interfere with the "impulsive and spontaneous" tendency of our will.

What's true of our spiritual and moral life is also true of our practical life. The "preponderance of nature over will" is evident in people of extraordinary achievement. "The best of their power was in nature," Emerson insists, "not in them."

> Their success lay in their parallelism to the course of thought, which found in them an unobstructed channel; and the wonders of which they were the visible conductors seemed to the eye their deed. Did the wires generate the galvanism? It is even true that there was less in them on which they could reflect than in another; as the virtue of a pipe is to be smooth and hollow.

These observations demonstrate the most basic spiritual laws, namely, "that our life might be much easier and simpler than we make it; that the world might be a happier place than it is; that there is no need of struggles, convulsions, and despairs, of the wringing of the hands and the gnashing of the teeth; that we miscreate our own evils." If not for our interference, we would find that "we are begirt with laws which execute themselves."

Nevertheless, we "fret and fume," to "intermeddle and have things in our own way," and to "pain ourselves to please nobody." Our Sunday schools, churches, and charities are all efforts to force morality where no force is needed. So much of society seems geared to engineer and constrict human behavior, when there are simpler and more natural ways to promote morality and spiritual growth:

> Let us draw a lesson from nature, which always works by short ways. When the fruit is ripe, it falls. When the fruit is dispatched, the leaf falls. The circuit of the waters is mere falling. The walking of man and all animals is a falling forward. All our manual labor and works of strength, as prying, splitting, digging, rowing and so forth, are done by dint of continual falling, and the globe, earth, moon, comet, sun, star, fall for ever and ever.

If we simply observe the method of nature we find that "a higher law than that of our will regulates events; that our painful labors are unnecessary and fruitless; that only in our easy, simple, spontaneous action are we strong, and by contenting ourselves with obedience we become divine." Emerson admonishes us to align ourselves with the natural course of things—what Chinese philosophers called the Tao, or the Way—and let it guide us in living a more effortless and spiritual life. The choices we make should be based on what's right for us, not on what others think we should do. They should be according to our own character and constitution. "Each man has his own vocation," Emerson argues. "The talent is the call. There is one direction in which all space is open to him. He has faculties guiding him thither to endless exertion. He is like a ship in a river; he runs against obstructions on every side but one, on that side all obstruction is taken away and he sweeps serenely over a deepening channel into an infinite sea. This talent and this call depend on his organization, or the mode in which the general soul incarnates itself in him."

We each have our own calling. If we follow a path not meant for us, we will experience frustration and not able to unfold ourselves as nature intends. Too often we pursue praiseworthy professions and fail to see that we might do something that only we can do.

Our genius, the quality that distinguishes us from everyone else, makes us susceptible to certain influences and determines for us the very character of the universe. "A man is a method, a progressive arrangement;" Emerson says, "a selecting principle, gathering his like to him wherever he goes. He takes only his own out of the multiplicity that sweeps and circles round him." All the things that attract our attention and become memorable for us relate to our gift. "What your heart thinks is great, is great. The soul's emphasis is always right."

We may take from experience only what belongs to our "spiritual estate." We cannot learn without readiness and preparation. "God screens us evermore from premature ideas," Emerson observes. "Our eyes are holden that we cannot see things that stare us in the face, until the hour arrives when the mind is ripened; then we behold them, and the time when we saw them was not like a dream." We impart meaning and significance to the world, not the other way around. We see what we are prepared to see.

The same is true of the company we keep. We seem to think that we can court friends by conforming to social expectations. "But only that soul can be my friend which I encounter on the line of my own march, that soul to which I do not decline and which does not decline to me . . ." If we assume the place and attitude that belong to us, others will accept us for who we are. And it's only when we rely on our own character and experience that we can teach or communicate with others. If we write from the heart, we find that we write to "an eternal public." There is no luck in literary reputation. Books last only by virtue of "the intrinsic importance of their contents to the constant mind of man."

The effect of every action is similarly measured by the depth of the sentiment from which it proceeds. Greatness may take time to be appreciated, but it depends on integrity. "Human character evermore publishes itself," Emerson alleges. "The most fugitive deed and word, the mere air of doing a thing, the intimated purpose, expresses character. If you act, you show character; if you sit still, if you sleep, you show it." In the end we pass for what we are worth. "The world is full of judgment-days, and into every assembly that a man enters, in every action he attempts, he is gauged and stamped."

Virtue consists in conforming our actions to the nature of things or, rather, in allowing the nature of things to have its way with us. Our ego is an obstacle. "The lesson which these observations convey is, Be, not seem. Let us acquiesce. Let us take our bloated nothingness out of the path of the divine circuits. Let us unlearn our wisdom of the world." If there's good to be done, we should do it now, without hesitation and without concern for appearances.

We esteem active pursuits more highly than contemplative ones. But our most profound and life-changing moments are those given to reflection; "real action is in silent moments." Emerson writes,

The epochs of our life are not in the visible facts of our choice of calling, our acquisition of an office, and the like, but in a silent thought by the wayside as we walk; in a thought which revises our entire manner of life and says,—'Thus hast thou done, but it were better thus.' And all our after years, like menials, serve and wait on this, and according to their ability to execute its will. This revisal or correction is a constant force, which, as a tendency, reaches through our lifetime. The object of the man, the aim of these moments, is to make daylight shine through him, to suffer the law to traverse his whole being without obstruction, so that on what point soever of his doing your eye falls it should report truly of his character, whether if be his diet, his house, his religious forms, his society, his mirth, his vote, his opposition.

We should not compare ourselves to others. We have our own gifts and talents and duties to accomplish. "I desire not to disgrace the soul," Emerson says. "The fact that I am here certainly shows me that the soul had need of an organ here. Shall I not assume the post?" When we do our own work, we find that the soul nourishes us and "unlocks new magazines of power and enjoyment" to us every day. It's not how we measure up to others, but how we measure up to our own potential that counts. The point is not to do what the great did, but to do our best. In that way our work, whatever it is, will be equal to theirs. "This over-estimate of Paul and Pericles, this underestimate of our own, comes from a neglect of the fact of an identical nature."

The soul is incarnated in every person. Even the work of chambermaids can appear "supreme and beautiful . . ., the top and radiance of human life." The great soul has enshrined itself in each of us, Emerson insists. "We are the photometers, we the irritable gold-leaf and tinfoil that measure the accumulations of the subtle element. We know the authentic effects of the true fire through every one of its million disguises."

Wu-wei is . . . the life-style of one who follows the Tao, and must be understood primarily as a form of intelligence—that is, of knowing the principles, structures, and trends of human and natural affairs so well that one uses the least amount of energy in dealing with them. But this intelligence is . . . not simply intellectual; is is also the "unconscious" intelligence of the whole organism and, in particular, the innate wisdom of the nervous system. Wu-wei is a combination of this wisdom with taking the line of least resistance in all one's actions.

—Alan Watts, *Tao*

When all a person's relevant skills are needed to cope with the challenges of a situation, that person's attention is completely absorbed by the activity. There is no excess psychic energy left over to process any information but what the activity offers. All the attention is concentrated on the relevant stimuli.

As a result, one of the most universal and distinctive features of optimal experience takes place: people become so involved in what they are doing that the activity becomes spontaneous, almost automatic; they stop being aware of themselves as separate from the activities they are performing.

It is for this reason that we called the optimal experience "flow." The short and simple word describes well the sense of seemingly effortless movement. . . . The purpose of flow is to keep on flowing, not looking for a peak or a utopia but staying in the flow. It is not a moving up but a continuous flowing; you move up to keep the flow going.

—Michael Csikszentmihalyi, *Flow*

Questions for Personal Reflection and Group Discussion

- How are you affected by Emerson's suggestion that you have never made a sacrifice or suffered pain?

- What does it mean to have a simple mind?

- Do you trust yourself sufficiently to be spontaneous in your actions?

- What is the essence of genius or extraordinary achievement in your view?

- To what extent do we "miscreate our own evils"?

- Would people be naturally virtuous if there were no churches and Sunday schools?

- What is your understanding of Taoism? Do you see any affinities between Taoism and Emerson's views in this essay?

- In your choice of vocation, do you feel that you have responded to a sense of calling or do that you have tried to fit yourself into what you have fallen into?

- Describe a "silent thought by the way-side" that you have had while you were out for a walk. Did it change you?

- Do you find that you overestimate the Pauls and Pericleses and underestimate yourself?

All goes to show that the soul in man is not an organ, but animates and exercises all the organs; is not a function, like the power of memory, of calculation, of comparison, but uses these as hands and feet; is not a faculty, but a light; is not the intellect or the will, but the master of the intellect and the will; is the background of our being, in which they lie,—an immensity not possessed and that cannot be possessed. From within or from behind, a light shines through us upon things and makes us aware that we are nothing, but the light is all.

"The Over-Soul," one of the most well-known essays from the 1841 series, is also the most mystical. It's an examination of those experiences that transform our lives by bringing us face to face with the nature of reality. Though intermittent and fleeting, they are full of significance. At such times we are aware that the soul in us is the manifestation of a universal soul. The sense of oneness we feel with the world gives coherence to our scattered and discordant lives. These experiences can't be summoned at will, but they can be encouraged by cultivating what Emerson calls an "attitude of reception" through contemplation and an appreciation of nature.

Emerson distinguishes mystical experience from ordinary experience. "Our faith comes in moments . . . our vice is habitual," he says. And yet there is a depth in those brief moments which constrains us to ascribe more reality to them than to all other experiences." Since the greater part of our lives is lived in the realm of the mundane, we are tempted to discount these extraordinary moments as abnormal. Nevertheless, they are judged to be of greater significance than everyday experiences.

In fact, they become the measure by which we find our lives wanting in depth and meaning. "What is the ground of this uneasiness of ours; of this old discontent?" Emerson asks. "The philosophy of six thousand years" hasn't been able to answer this question because it hasn't yet examined "the chambers and magazines of the soul." If we but searched the soul, we'd discover that "man is a stream whose source is hidden. Our being is descending into us from we know not whence." This discovery constrains us to acknowledge "a higher origin for events" than our own will:

> When I watch that flowing river, which, out of regions I see not, pours for a season its streams into me, I see that I am not a pensioner; not a cause, but a surprised spectator of this ethereal water; that I desire and look up, and put myself in the attitude of reception, but from some alien energy the visions come.

The source Emerson speaks of is "that great nature in which we rest as the earth lies in the soft arms of the atmosphere; that Unity, that Over-Soul, within which every man's particular being is contained and made one with all other." We live divided, partial, and piecemeal lives. Yet within each of us is "the soul of the whole; the wise silence; the universal beauty, to which every part and particle is equally related; the eternal *One*."

Emerson's notion is very much like the Hindu conception of *Brahma*, or world soul, which is identified with the individual soul, or *atman*. As Emerson says, "We see the world piece by piece, as the sun, the moon, the animal, the tree; but the whole, of which these are the shining parts, is the soul." Insight into this oneness is the highest sort of wisdom that humans can aspire to, and it's intuitively available to each of us. This may be difficult to explain to one who hasn't had such an experience, but Emerson attests to the truth of what he has witnessed.

The individual soul, which, as Emerson says, is part and parcel of the oversoul, is not a physical entity, but a spiritual reality. Most of what we do as human beings—working, eating, reading, walking, and so on—is incidental to our being. What's essential is the soul, whose organ we are. "When it breathes through [man's] intellect, it is genius; when it breathes through his will, it is virtue; when it flows through his affection, it is love."

At some time or another, we are all aware of the truth of Emerson's remarks. We are, after all, spiritual beings who know intuitively that "as there is no screen or ceiling between our heads and the infinite heavens, so there is no bar or wall in the soul where man, the effect, ceases, and God, the cause, begins." The soul is unlimited; it "circumscribes all things" and "abolishes time and space." When we are caught up in the realm of the soul, we feel renewed and youthful, redeemed "from the conditions of time." This is the experience of the eternal now: "Before the revelations of the soul, Time, Space, and Nature shrink away." By comparison, everything else seems transitory and ephemeral. "The soul knows only the soul," Emerson insists, and "the web of events is the flowing robe in which she is clothed."

The growth of the soul happens by a process of transformation or metamorphosis, as from the egg to the worm, the worm to the fly. One of these forms is that of a social person, in relationship to others. We discover that there's a third party to all such relationships: "In all conversation between two persons, tacit reference is made, as to a third party, to a common nature. That third party or common nature is not social; it is impersonal; is God." This is why there is more wisdom in the group than in the individual:

> They all become wiser than they were. It arches over them like a temple, this unity of thought, in which every heart beats with nobler sense of power and duty, and thinks and acts with unusual solemnity. All are conscious of attaining to a higher self-possession.

Our customary relations with others are seldom on such a high plane, and therefore, as Emerson says, "men descend to meet."

As the soul is present in all persons, it is also present at every stage of life, including childhood, leading Emerson to insist, "In my dealing with my child, my Latin and Greek, my accomplishments and my money stead me nothing; but as much soul as I have avails." Instead of a war of wills with our children, we should propose a meeting of souls, since essentially we share the same soul.

The soul is its own authority. It's by virtue of the soul that we know the truth when we see it. We are always wiser than we know, and if we didn't interfere with our own thought, we would know more than we do. Revelations are intuitions of the soul, attended by the emotion of the sublime. Such "communication is an influx of the Divine mind into our mind. It is an ebb of the individual rivulet before the flowing surges of the sea of life. Every distinct apprehension of this central commandment agitates men with awe and delight." We feel energized by these revelations: "Every moment when the individual feels himself invaded by it is memorable. By the necessity of our constitution a certain enthusiasm attends the individual's consciousness of that divine presence." They vary in their duration and intensity, from ecstasy, trance, and prophetic inspiration to "the faintest glow of virtuous emotion." In some people they may seem like a form of insanity. "Everywhere the history of religion betrays a tendency to enthusiasm."

But the nature of these revelations is always the same; namely, "they are perceptions of the absolute law." They are answers to the soul's own questions, not to questions posed by the senses. "Revelation is the disclosure of the soul." The revelations of the soul are not predictions, premonitions, or prophesies:

> Do not require a description of the countries towards which you sail. The description does not describe them to you, and to-morrow you arrive there, and know them by inhabiting them. Men ask concerning the immortality of the soul, the employments of heaven, the state of the sinner, and so forth. They even dream that Jesus has left replies to precisely these interrogatories. Never a moment did that sublime spirit speak in their *patois*.

To assume that eternity has anything to do with duration in a temporal sense is to commit what philosopher Alfred North Whitehead called "the fallacy of misplaced concreteness," confusing the spiritual with the material. For those who wonder about such things as life after death, Emerson has this to say:

> The only mode of obtaining an answer to these questions of the senses is to forego all low curiosity, and, accepting the tide of being which floats us into the secret of nature, work and live, work and live, and all unawares the advancing soul has built and forged for itself a new condition, and the question and the answer are one.

Issues regarding character are also to be resolved holistically, as wholes that can't be separated into component parts. "That which we are, we shall teach, not voluntarily, but involuntarily," Emerson says. "Character teaches over our head."

The primary distinction between philosophers and religious teachers is that some speak from within, or from experience, while others speak from without, "as spectators merely," or at third hand. "It is of no use to preach to me from without," Emerson argues. "I can do that too easily myself." Genius, which is essentially spiritual in nature, is the flowing of omniscience into the intellect. "It is a larger imbibing of the common heart." It makes us more, not less, like others. It's the sine qua non of the true spiritual teacher, and it's freely available to any who will observe its strict conditions:

> This energy does not descend into individual life on any other condition than entire possession. It comes to the lowly and simple; it comes to whomsoever will put off what is foreign and proud; it comes as insight; it comes as serenity and grandeur. . . . It requires of us to be plain and true.

Some people try to impress by name-dropping, some by showing off their possessions, others by embellishing their experiences. The enlightened soul puts on no airs and doesn't seek admiration, but only "dwells in the hour that now is, in the earnest experience of the common day."

The influx of the soul is ever new and unsearchable. It is astonishing and awe-inspiring. It is here and now for those who dispense with the gods of tradition and rhetoric. When we are ready for this experience, all things will work in our favor. "Every proverb, every

69

book, every byword that belongs to thee for aid or comfort, shall surely come home through open or winding passages." This is so because everything is connected: "the heart in thee is the heart of all; not a valve, not a wall, not an intersection is there anywhere in nature, but one blood rolls uninterruptedly an endless circulation through all men, as the water of the globe is all one sea, and, truly seen, its tide is one."

Both intuition and the experience of nature reveal to us that the highest dwells within. But we know this only if we seek contemplation in solitude, withdrawing ourselves "from all the accents of other men's devotion." The appeal to numbers is no basis for religion. The faith that stands on the authority of others is not faith. Reliance on authority indicates the decline of religion and the loss of the soul. We must rely on ourselves. "Great is the soul, and plain," Emerson insists. "It is no flatterer, it is no follower; it never appeals from itself. It believes in itself."

The soul gives itself to those who are open to receive it. Its reception makes us one with "the universal mind." In its presence we feel "the surges of everlasting nature." We come "to live in thoughts and act with energies that are immortal." In the rapture of the soul, we "will come to see that the world is the perennial miracle that the soul worketh," that the world is not profane but sacred, and that "the universe is represented in an atom, in a moment of time." Most importantly, we "will weave no longer a spotted life of shreds and patches, but . . . will live with a divine unity."

Underlying the human self and animating it is a reservoir of being that never dies, is never exhausted, and is unrestricted in consciousness and bliss. This infinite center of every life, this hidden self or Atman, is no less than Brahman, the Godhead.

—Huston Smith, *The World's Religions*

We pass into mystical states from out of ordinary consciousness as from a less into a more, as from a smallness into a vastness, and at the same time as from an unrest to a rest. We feel them as reconciling, unifying states. . . . This overcoming of all the usual barriers between the individual and the Absolute is the great mystic achievement. In mystic states we become one with the Absolute and we become aware of our oneness. This is the everlasting and triumphant mystical traditions, hardly altered by differences of clime or creed.

—William James, *Varieties of Religious Experience*

Questions for Personal Reflection and Group Discussion

- Describe a moment that was more significant to you than everyday experiences? Did it change the way you looked at your life or the world?

- How would you choose to describe the nature of Being or the Absolute? Do you find Emerson's terms helpful? What are your preferred terms?

- When and under what conditions have you had an experience of the Eternal Now?

- Given William James's description of mystical experiences, would you say that Emerson is alluding to the same thing? Do you think the essence of religion is mysticism?

- Emerson felt that mysticism had nothing to do with magic, oracles, or fortune-telling. Would you agree?

- Does Emerson impress you as a religious teacher who speaks from within, from experience, or from without, as a spectator merely?

- Do you feel that most of the time we live "a spotted life of shreds and patches?" In your experience, do such moments as Emerson describes bring with them a feeling of wholeness and harmony?

CIRCLES

The life of man is a self-evolving circle, which, from a ring imperceptibly small, rushes on all sides outwards to new and larger circles, and that without end. The extent to which this generation of circles, wheel without wheel, will go, depends on the force or truth of the individual soul. For it is the inert effort of each thought, having formed itself into a circular wave of circumstance,—as, for instance, an empire, rules of an art, a local usage, a religious rite,—to heap itself on that ridge, and to solidify and hem in life. But if the soul is quick and strong, it bursts over that boundary on all sides, and expands another orbit on the great deep, which also runs up into a high wave, with attempt again to stop and to bind. But the heart refuses to be imprisoned; in its first and narrowest pulses, it already tends outward with a vast force, and to immense and innumerable expansions.

Among Emerson's first series *Essays* (1841), "Circles" is not as widely read or commented on as the more popular "Self-Reliance" and "The Over-Soul." Yet this essay is important because it provides a Transcendentalist model for spiritual growth. It emphasizes spiritual development as a process of continual transformation, of expansion outward, in the same way that paradigms shift as a result of new insights. There's no end state in Emerson's view of the spiritual life. All things—ideas, institutions, inventions—are in a state of change and flux. There's a natural conservative tendency to arrest change in the latest formulation of the truth, but Emerson insists that it's only by embracing change that there's any hope for us. There's power, excitement, and vitality in the transition from one paradigm to another. This expansion outward might be disconcerting if not for our inner core, the soul, which is eternal and unchanging and keeps us grounded. It's Emerson's view that when we are grounded in the soul, we may abandon ourselves to the flux of things without fear or confusion.

Emerson begins by noting the prevalence of circles in nature, leading Emerson to conclude that the circle is "the highest emblem in the cipher of the world." It also provides an analogy for human thought and action. Every thought and action can be outdone. "Our life is an apprenticeship to the truth, that around every circle another can be drawn; that there is no end in nature, but every end is a beginning; that there is always another dawn risen on mid-noon, and under every deep a lower deep opens."

The fact that every circle can be encompassed by a new one symbolizes the nature of being itself, "the Unattainable, the flying Perfect, around which the hands of man can never meet, at once the inspirer and the condemner of every success." The symbolism of circles is also characteristic of nature and human culture and gives rise to a doctrine of impermanence. "There are no fixtures in nature," Emerson insists. "The universe is fluid and volatile. Permanence is but a word of degrees. . . . Our culture is the predominance of an idea which draws after it this train of cities and institutions. Let us rise into another idea; they will disappear. . . . New arts destroy the old." Everything is eventually superceded by something else.

Human beings cling to ideas that seem to give coherence to the world of their experience. The only way to reform them is to introduce a new idea. Emerson explains this model for spiritual development. Everything we think of as ultimate and final turns out to be the beginning of something new. "Every general law only a particular fact of some more general law presently to disclose itself. There is no outside, no inclosing wall, no circumference to us." No matter how comprehensive an idea seems to be, it eventually becomes an example of an even bolder generalization. Therefore ideas are not only impermanent but progressive in the sense that new ones are successively grander in scale and significance. "In the thought of tomorrow there is a power to upheave all thy creed, all the creeds, all the literatures, of the nations, and marshal thee to a heaven which no epic dream has yet depicted."

Such enlargements of thought are accompanied by an increase of power as well. "Step by step we scale this mysterious ladder: the steps are actions; the new prospect is power." Yet we hesitate to embrace the new. We are used to the old and the customary and feel threatened by the new. "Resist it not," Emerson insists. There is or should be something unknowable about us, otherwise we have no potential for growth or change. "The last chamber, the last closet, he must feel, was never opened; there is always a residuum unknown, unanalyzable. That is, every man believes that he has a greater possibility."

We find it hard to imagine that things could be other than they are. Yet we find, for example, that where once we felt unproductive, now we wonder that we could have accomplished so much. We should have more confidence. "Alas for this infirm faith, this will not strenuous, this vast ebb of a vast flow! I am God in nature; I am a weed by the wall." Ours should be a continual effort to raise ourselves above ourselves, "to work a pitch above [our] last height." Those who fail to do so lose interest for us. "The only sin is limitation." Of such people Emerson says, "Infinitely alluring and attractive was he to you yesterday, a great hope, a sea to swim in; now, you have found his shores, found it a pond, and you care not if you never see it again."

The thinking of great minds reconciles opposing ideas, gathering up "seemingly discordant facts" into a new synthesis of a unified theory. In the process old thinking is turned upside down. "Beware when the great God lets loose a thinker on this planet," Emerson warns his readers. "Then all things are set at risk." There's no scientific theory or literary reputation that's not at the mercy of a new generalization. "Generalization is always a new influx of the divinity into the mind. Hence the thrill that attends it."

The only thing for us is to be open to the possibility of the new and to embrace it when it comes. "Valor consists in the power of self-recovery," Emerson insists, "so that a man cannot have his flank turned, cannot be out-generalled, but put him where you will, he stands." This can be done only by preferring truth to any past expression of it, knowing that even strong convictions will eventually be supplanted by new ones. Ideas that we consider important once emerged on the horizon and helped us understand the present order of things. This is as natural as a tree bearing apples. Nevertheless, a "new degree of culture," by which Emerson means transformation or spiritual growth, "would instantly revolutionize the entire system of human pursuits."

Conversation is an example of the way in which new ideas grow out of, encompass, and finally supercede the old. "When each new speaker strikes a new light, emancipates us from the oppression of the last speaker, to oppress us with the greatness and exclusiveness of his own thought, then yields us to another redeemer, we seem to recover our rights, to become men." It's the same with all things that loom so large in our minds: "property, climate, breeding, personal beauty and the like" are all subject to revision. "All that we reckoned settled shakes and rattles; and literatures, cities, climates, religions, leave their foundations and dance before our eyes."

The natural world may be seen as a process or progression. It too is "not fixed, but sliding." Animals, vegetables, and minerals, "which seem to stand there for their own sake," are merely means and methods. This "law of eternal progression" applies to the moral world as well, extinguishing past virtues in light of better ones. What was one person's justice becomes another's injustice, one person's wisdom, another's folly, as these are viewed from a higher vantage point. "There is no virtue which is final," Emerson observes; "all are initial."

It's a frightening prospect—"the terror of reform," as Emerson puts it—that what we have esteemed to be virtues must be thrown into the same pit as our vices. Even our contritions are dissolved in the light of "divine moments" that change our outlook on life:

> I accuse myself of sloth and unprofitableness day by day; but when these waves of God flow into me I no longer reckon lost time. I no longer poorly compute my possible achievement by what remains to

me of the month or the year; for these moments confer a sort of omnipresence and omnipotence which asks nothing of duration, but sees that the energy of the mind is commensurate with the work to be done, without time.

If everything changes, is there nothing we can hold onto? Is truth finally unattainable? Have we arrived at "an equivalence and indifferency of all actions?" In reply, Emerson insists that he is only an experimenter:

> Do not set the least value on what I do, or the least discredit on what I do not, as if I pretended to settle any thing as true or false. I unsettle all things. No facts are to me sacred; none are profane; I simply experiment, an endless seeker, with no Past at my back.

Yet we could never be aware of "this incessant movement and progression which all things partake" if not in contrast "to some principle of fixture or stability in the soul" itself. "Whilst the eternal generation of circles proceeds, the eternal generator abides." The central life of the soul is superior to knowledge and thought and "contains all its circles."

Things rush on: "there is no sleep, no pause, no preservation, but all things renew, germinate and spring." Nature has no room for the old. Rest, conservatism, inertia are forms of old age. These are "not newness, not the way onward." Though we seem to "grizzle" a little every day, there's no need to. "Whilst we converse with what is above us, we do not grow old, but grow young." Therefore, let us become "organs of the Holy Ghost." Our eyes will be uplifted, our wrinkles smoothed, and we will be "perfumed again with hope and power." Old age ought not afflict the human mind.

> In nature every moment is new; the past is always swallowed and forgotten; the coming only is sacred. Nothing is secure but life, transition, the energizing spirit. . . . No truth so sublime but it may be trivial to-morrow in the light of new thoughts. People wish to be settled; only as far as they are unsettled is there any hope for them.

"Life," Emerson says, "is a series of surprises." The routines of daily life are predictable enough, "but the masterpieces of God, the total growths and universal movements of the soul," these are incalculable. We can never know where the pursuit of the truth will lead us. Such a position or posture "carries in its bosom all the energies of the past, yet is itself an exhalation of the morning." But it requires an ability to let go of our need for surety and security:

> The one thing which we seek with insatiable desire is to forget ourselves, to be surprised out of our propriety, to lose our sempertinal memory and to do something without knowing how or why; in short to draw a new circle. Nothing great was ever achieved without enthusiasm. The way of life is wonderful; it is by abandonment.

You have noticed that everything an Indian does is in a circle, and that is because the Power of the World always works in circles, and everything tries to be round. In the old days when we were a strong and happy people, all our power came to us from the sacred hoop of the nation, and so long as the hoop was unbroken, the people flourished. The flowering tree was the living center of the hoop, and the circle of the four quarters nourished it. . . . Everything the Power of the World does is in a circle. The sky is round, and I have heard that the earth is round like a ball, and so are all the stars. The wind, in its greatest power, whirls. Birds make their nests in circles, for theirs is the same religion as ours.

—John G. Neihardt, *Black Elk Speaks*

Transition renews us. It is as though the breakdown of the old reality releases energy that has been trapped in the form of our old lives and converts it back into its original state of pure and formless energy. It is recapturing that energy that permits us to be reborn anew—as in the old rites of passage, the person was put through a symbolic experience of being born all over again. . . . Then—but only then—can we come out of what is really a death-and-rebirth process with a new identity, a new sense of purpose, and a new store of life energy. . . . Renewal is possible only by going into and through transition, and transition always has at least as much to do with what we let go of as it has whatever we end up gaining in its place.

—William Bridges, *The Way of Transition*

Questions for Personal Reflection and Group Discussion

- Have you ever experienced a radical transformation in your own life or thinking? How did you find the experience? Frightening? Confusing? Exhilarating?

- Can you think of instances in the history of human thought when one idea was superceded by another? Was there resistance to change?

- Is the circle a useful image for you in terms of your own spiritual growth?

- Emerson feels that a great deal of power and energy is unleashed in the transition from one set of ideas to another. Do you agree? Have you experienced new strength and vitality as a result of changes in your point of view?

- Do you typically resist new ideas or rush to embrace them? Do you find that your openness to new ideas changes as you grow older?

- If everything changes, is there nothing to hold on to? What would you hold on to?

- "The way of life is wonderful," Emerson says; "it is by abandonment." Do you agree? Would you say that you live your life as though this were true? Has this ever been true for you?

THE TRANSCENDENTALIST

[My faith is] a certain brief experience, which surprised me in the highway or in the market, in some place, at some time,—whether in the body or out of the body, God knoweth—and made me aware that I had played the fool with fools all this time, but that law existed for me and for all; that to me belonged trust, a child's trust and obedience, and the worship of ideas, and I should never be fool more. Well, in the space of an hour probably, I was let down from this height; I was at my old tricks, the selfish member of a selfish society. My life is superficial, takes no root in the deep world; I ask, When shall I die and be relieved of the responsibility of seeing an Universe which I do not use? I wish to exchange this flash-of-lightning faith for continuous daylight, this fever glow for a benign climate.

Emerson delivered "The Transcendentalist" at the Masonic Temple in Boston in January 1842, a little less than six years after the formation of the Transcendental Club. Many of its members either were or like Emerson, had been Unitarian ministers. In fact, Transcendentalism represented a revolt within the ranks of "orthodox" Unitarianism. By the time the lecture was given, the Transcendentalists had already attracted considerable attention through their writings and speeches. They had also founded a commune, Brook Farm, and produced a magazine, *The Dial.* Emerson, foremost among them, had by this time published two books, *Nature* and the first series of *Essays*, and delivered numerous lectures and addresses, including the controversial "Divinity School Address."

If we didn't know that Emerson was the central figure in this movement, we might assume from reading this lecture that he was an outside observer. He talks about it as though he wasn't necessarily a part of it. But we know better. He first points out that "new views" in New England are not in fact new, "but the very oldest of thoughts cast into the mould of these new times."

"What is popularly called Transcendentalism among us, is Idealism," Emerson insists; "Idealism as it appears in 1842." He contrasts idealism with materialism, contending that materialism is based on experience, idealism on consciousness. He makes essentially the same distinction between reason and understanding. Reason, for Emerson and the Transcendentalists, means intuition. Understanding represents empirical knowledge, or measurable facts. The Transcendentalist doesn't deny the world of facts, but does not stop there. Besides a fact itself, there is the consideration of what it means to us, what we make of it, the value it has, and the reality it assumes in our minds. Truth, known by intuition, through consciousness, is greater than facts derived empirically from experience. Materialism never has the final word.

The materialist, says Emerson, only thinks he stands on solid ground. Though the materialist mocks "at star-gazers and dreamers," he is himself a "phantom":

> The sturdy capitalist, no matter how deep and square on blocks of Quincy granite he lays the foundations of his banking-house or Exchange, must set it, at last, not on a cube corresponding to the angles of his structure, but on a mass of unknown materials and solidity, red-hot or white-hot perhaps at the core, which rounds off to an almost perfect sphericity, and lies floating in soft air, and goes spinning away, dragging bank and banker with it at a rate of thousands of miles the hour, he knows not whither,—a bit of bullet, now glimmering, now darkling through a small cubic space on the edge of an unimaginable pit of emptiness.

The materialist thinks that the world of experience is solid and uniform, but his faith in figures is no more secure than the "quaking foundations" of the sturdy capitalist's edifice of stone.

For the Transcendentalist it is mind, not matter, that is the only true reality, because it's the mind that assigns things the rank or importance they assume in our consciousness:

> His thought,—that is the Universe. His experience inclines him to behold the procession of facts you call the world, as flowing perpetually outward from an invisible, unsounded centre in himself, centre alike of him and of them, and necessitating him to regard all things as having a subjective or relative existence, relative to that aforesaid Unknown Centre of him.

Mind, or consciousness, is self-dependent or, in the title of his most famous essay, self-reliant. The world is the shadow of the substance we think we are, "the perpetual creation of the powers of thought." We are not passive recipients of knowledge or victims of circumstance; we make our own realities. "Let the soul be erect, and all things will go well," Emerson says. "Let any thought or motive of mine be different from that they are, the difference will transform my condition and economy."

The Transcendentalist takes a spiritual point of view, believing in miracle, inspiration, and ecstasy, "in the perpetual openness of the human mind to a new influx of light and power." Hence the Transcendentalist is essentially a mystic. Emerson denies that there can be any such thing as a Transcendental *party* or even a pure Transcendentalist. Though there have been many forerunners of a purely spiritual life, we have had none yet who could live entirely on "angels' food," taking no thought for tomorrow. Transcendentalism is a form of spirituality, according to Emerson, a "Saturnalia or excess of Faith" that has produced idealists, as opposed to materialists, in every age.

The term *Transcendental* comes from the philosophy of Immanuel Kant. Like the American Transcendentalists, Kant was opposed to the philosophy of John Locke, who held that there was nothing in the intellect that was not first in the senses. Kant argued that there were innate ideas, "intuitions of the mind itself," which he termed "transcendental forms." Thus, even if there is no pure Transcendentalist, "the tendency to respect the intuitions and to give them, at least in our creed, all authority over our experience, has deeply colored the conversation and poetry of the present day; and the history of genius and of religion in these times, though impure, and as yet not incarnated in any powerful individual, will be the history of this tendency."

As a reaction to the materialism and commercialism of their day, many would-be Transcendentalists pursued "a certain solitary and critical way," holding themselves aloof, at once shunning what society expects of them and crying out for something worthy to do. But as Americans are ever in a hopeful mood, "whoso knows these seething brains, these admirable radicals, these unsocial worshippers, these talkers who talk the sun and moon away, will believe that this heresy cannot pass away without leaving its mark." The same could be said of the radicals of the 1960s, who had much in common with those of the 1830s.

Being a countercultural movement, the Transcendentalists incurred the censure of society, which interprets their aloofness as disapproval. However, these young men and women are not by nature unsocial or melancholy. To the contrary, they are "joyous, susceptible, affectionate." They wish to be loved, but they have high expectations of others. "Their quarrel with every man they meet, is not with his kind, but with his degree," as Emerson puts it. "There is not enough of him,—that is the only fault." In their idealism, they extract a harsh judgment of others, particularly their elders:

> Where are the old idealists? where are they who represented to the last generation that extravagant hope, which a few happy aspirants suggest to ours? . . . Are they dead. . . . Or did the high idea die out of them, and leave their unperfumed body as its tomb and tablet, announcing to all that the celestial inhabitant, who once gave them beauty, had departed? Will it be better with the new generation?

Because they are so exacting of others and repelled by the superficiality of human relations, they are inclined to withdraw from society. "They do not even like to vote," Emerson observes. Even the reformers and philanthropists are inclined to consider them dropouts: "they had as lief hear that their friend is dead, as that he is a Transcendentalist; for then is he paralyzed, and can never do anything for humanity." The youth reply that these "great and holy causes"—Abolition, Temperance, Unitarianism—soon become institutionalized and compromised, and the life goes out of them. What they want is integrity, not hypocrisy. "If I cannot work, at least I need not lie," he imagines them saying. "All that is clearly due today is not to lie."

What's going on with them is that they are trying to remain true to a mystical insight that has made a deep impression on them. Mystical experiences such as these are at once profound and transitory. The greatest challenge of the spiritual life is to integrate these fleeting moments—full of wonder and significance—with the realities of everyday life.

It's a recurring theme in Emerson's writing, often referred to as the problem of "double consciousness." We seem to live two lives that bear little relation to each other. "One prevails now, all buzz and din; and the other prevails then, all infinitude and paradise; and, with the progress of life, the two discover no greater disposition to reconcile themselves." We have these moments of enlightenment only briefly before "the clouds shut down again." Nevertheless, "we retain the belief that this petty web we weave will at last be overshot and reticulated with veins of the blue, and that the moments will characterize the days."

Emerson accepts some of the criticism that is leveled against the Transcendentalists. Inevitably, he says, there "will be cant and pretension; there will be subtilty and moonshine." There are inconsistencies (as though there are none among the guardians of civic virtue). But they are young, Emerson says, and may be excused their excesses. Better that they "obey the Genius then most when his impulse is wildest." Society has an obligation to them too. Besides "farmers, sailors, and weavers," there must also be "collectors of the heavenly spark with power to convey the electricity to others." Society needs idealists who speak "for thoughts and principles not marketable or perishable." The thoughts these nonconformists sought to proclaim "not only by what they did, but by what they forbore to do," shall enable us to achieve a "fuller union with the surrounding system," long after commercial improvements and mechanical inventions have outlived their usefulness.

⟨ॐ⟩

Mystical states cannot be sustained for long. Except in rare instances, half an hour, or at most an hour or two, seems to be the limit beyond which they fade into the light of common day. Often, when faded, their quality can but imperfectly be reproduced in memory; but when they recur it is recognized; and from one recurrence to another it is susceptible of continuous development in what is felt as inner richness and importance.

—William James, *The Varieties of Religious Experience*

Enlightenment does exist. It is possible to awaken. Unbounded freedom and joy, oneness with the Divine, awakening into a state of timeless grace—these experiences are more common than you know, and not far away. There is one further truth, however: They don't last. Our realizations and awakenings show us the reality of the world, and they bring transformation, but they pass. . . . We all know that after the honeymoon comes the marriage, after the election comes the hard task of governance. In spiritual life it is the same: After ecstasy comes the laundry.

—Jack Kornfield, *After the Ecstasy, the Laundry*

Questions for Personal Reflection and Group Discussion

- Would you say that you are an idealist or a materialist, in Emerson's use of these terms? How would you characterize the difference between the two?

- Do you share Emerson's essentially mystical view of religion? Do you consider yourself a religious mystic?

- Do you see any similarities between the counterculture of the 1960s and the young Transcendentalists Emerson speaks of?

- Do you ever feel that your life is superficial and "takes no root in the deep world"? Have you ever had an experience of feeling in union with the rest of the world such as Emerson describes?

- How are you able to integrate "infinitude and paradise" with the realities of everyday life? Is this a spiritual issue for you?

- Is there an important role that principled nonconformists play in society? Do you consider yourself a conformist or nonconformist? Where do you place yourself on that spectrum?

EXPERIENCE

To finish the moment, to find the journey's end in every step of the road, to live the greatest number of good hours, is wisdom. It is not the part of men, but of fanatics, or of mathematicians, if you will, to say that, the shortness of life considered, it is not worth caring whether for so short a duration we were sprawling in want, or sitting high. Since our office is with moments, let us husband them. Five minutes of today are worth as much to me, as five minutes in the next millennium.... Without any shadow of doubt, amidst this vertigo of shows and politics, I settle myself ever the firmer in the creed, that we should not postpone and refer and wish, but do broad justice where we are, by whomsoever we deal with, accepting our actual companions and circumstances, however humble or odious, as the mystic officials to whom the universe has delegated its whole pleasure for us.

"Experience" is a difficult, sometimes painful essay to read. Not only is it challenging to follow Emerson's train of thought, but the essay is deeply introspective and, at times, melancholy. Emerson's earlier essays seem much more self-assured and affirmative by comparison. Written in the period of 1843 to 1844, this essay represents a departure—some say a turning point—in Emerson's philosophy of life. It begins on a note reminiscent of the opening lines of Dante's *Divine*

Comedy, as if to suggest a midlife assessment of our spiritual condition. "Where do we find ourselves?" Emerson asks. Stranded apparently somewhere between the beginning and end of life. We feel adrift, lethargic, and enervated, having only enough strength to get by from day to day. It's as though someone has cut off the source of our spiritual energies.

The days leave a residue of accomplishments, to be sure, but on the whole, "our life looks trivial." So much of our time is spent in preparation and routine that "the pith of each man's genius contracts itself to a very few hours." There's no tangible result to our efforts, only "the most slippery, sliding surfaces." Our moods and emotions, even our relationships, seem evanescent. Emerson can't even hold on to the grief he felt at the death of his son only two years before.

As a younger man Emerson's spiritual life had oscillated between the poles of mystical insight and mundane reality, what he often referred to as the dilemma of "double consciousness." With the loss of innocence, his youthful confidence gone, he finds himself at midlife lost in a dark wood of doubt and confusion. The essay is called "Experience" because it's in the world of everyday experience that Emerson finds himself trapped. If he's ever to recover what he refers to as "the affirmative principle" and achieve a sense of balance and wholeness in life, it will be in and through this world of experience. Emerson struggles to develop a perspective that might reconcile his earlier faith with his newfound skepticism. At this stage of his life, he feels the need to revise his philosophy in a way that will acknowledge life's limitations, as well as celebrate its possibilities. Without surrendering his habitual optimism, he wants to articulate a more realistic sense of life.

In this attempt Emerson examines each of the conditions of human existence, which he terms "the lords of life": Illusion, Temperament, Succession, Surface, Surprise, Reality, and Subjectiveness. The first of these "lords" is Illusion, the sense that nothing is at last real or permanent. Life slips through our fingers even (perhaps especially) when we clutch hardest. Life is a succession of moods that inevitably affect the way we see things.

Temperament—the second lord—rescues us from illusion and subjectivity. Temperament is something more substantial. However, we find that we substitute a form of determinism for what had seemed hopelessly subjective. It confines us in "a prison of glass which we cannot see" and "prevails over everything of time, place, and condition." Ultimately, it leaves no room for the spirit, reducing intangible qualities such as love and faith to a medical materialism akin to phrenology (the prediction of a person's future based on the shape of his head).

We are freed from the constraints of materialism because temperament itself has its limits. Seen from within, the determinism seems complete: "Given such an embryo, such a history must follow." But seen from without, there are always the seeds of change. "It is impossible that the creative power should exclude itself," Emerson insists. "Into every intelligence there is a door which is never closed, through which the creator passes." In Emerson's view, spirit is greater than matter. Faith and love are more powerful than the determinism of temperament. "At one whisper of these high powers, we awake from ineffectual struggles with this nightmare. We hurl it into its own hell, and cannot again contract ourselves to so base a state."

Succession, the third of the lords, is the evidence of the limitation of determinism. There's no end to change. "Our love of the real draws us to permanence," Emerson says, "but health of body consists in circulation, and sanity of mind in variety or facility of association. We need change of objects. Dedication to one thought is quickly odious." Without change, there can be no growth. People become predictable and stuck in their ways, and in doing so, they limit their powers: "They stand on the brink of the ocean of thought and power, but they never take the single step that would bring them there."

Each person has a contribution to make; each one is an outcropping of genius in the world. Society can only be whole and complete if it accepts what each individual has to offer. "Like a bird which alights nowhere, but hops perpetually from bough to bough," Emerson writes, "is the Power which abides in no man and in no woman, but for a moment speaks from this one, and for another moment from that one."

For one who was notorious for being abstract, Emerson's thinking becomes increasingly practical and pragmatic. "Life is not dialectics," he insists. Young people want to change the world, but the "intellectual tasting of life will not supersede muscular activity." In a reference to activities at Brook Farm, he notes that "the noblest theory of life" does "not rake or pitch a ton of hay." Self-culture that is merely academic "ends in headache." Life is not a problem to be solved, but a course of action to be taken, knowing that life consists of any number of possibilities. What's important is to "fill the hour—that is happiness; to fill the hour and leave no crevice for a repentance or an approval."

Surface is the next lord that Emerson encounters on his quest through the world of experience. "We live amid surfaces," he says, "and the true art of life is to skate well on them." Emerson is suggesting that we try to achieve moderation and balance in life. "Life itself," he says, "is a mixture of power and form, and will not bear the least excess of either." Young people expect too much of life and are easily disappointed. Emerson's aspirations are more modest: ". . . leave me alone and I should relish every hour and what it brought me, the pot-luck of the day, as heartily as the oldest gossip in the barroom." He is "thankful for small mercies." Compared with those with high expectations and low levels of satisfaction, Emerson starts at the other end, "expecting nothing, and . . . always full of thanks for moderate goods."

Emerson finds meaning in the realities of everyday life, accepting "the clangor and jangle of contrary tendencies," finding his "account in sots and bores also." He finds satisfaction in the world of familiar associations:

> In the morning I awake, and find the old world, wife, babes and mother, Concord and Boston, the dear old spiritual world, and even the dear old devil not far off. If we will take the good we find, asking no questions, we shall have heaping measures. The great gifts are not got by analysis. Everything good is on the highway. The middle region of our being is the temperate zone. We may climb into the thin and cold realm of pure geometry and lifeless science, or sink into that of sensation. Between these extremes is the equator of life, of thought, of spirit, of poetry,—a narrow belt.

We don't need to shop for paintings; we can see them in the museum, to say nothing of being able to appreciate "nature's pictures in every street, of sunsets and sunrises every day." Collectors pay good money for Shakespeare's autograph, but a student can profit from reading Hamlet without paying a cent. Life consists of savoring what the world offers so freely and indiscriminately to all. "Nature is no saint," Emerson says. Her favorites are not the moralists, but those who commit themselves to living life to its fullest.

Surface gives way to Surprise in the sequence of Emerson's lords of life. It may represent wisdom to attempt to achieve harmony and balance in life. "We might keep forever these beautiful limits, and adjust ourselves, once for all, to the perfect calculation of the kingdom of known cause and effect," but fate doesn't allow us to do so. "But ah!" Emerson observes, "presently comes a day, or is it only a half-hour, with its angel-whispering,—which discomfits the conclusions of nations and of years."

Things may return to normal soon enough, but history and human life is a record of the disruptions of the status quo. "Power keeps quite another road than the turnpikes of choice and will," Emerson insists, "namely, the subterranean and invisible tunnels and channels of life." We are dupes to think that we can skate on the surface of life and lead an entirely moderate form of existence. "Life is a series of surprises," he says, "and would not be worth taking or keeping, if it were not." Life is essentially unpredictable. Serendipity, spontaneity, and novelty are necessary qualities of human existence, without which life would be dull and repetitive. "In the thought of genius there is always a surprise. . . . Every man is an impossibility, until he is born; every thing is impossible, until we see a success."

Nature itself is impulsive. Its methods are "undulatory and alternate." Power, which is a necessary force in all creation and creativity, surges throughout the universe, animating nature and energizing the human mind. There is an element of grace in the world that can't be denied:

I would gladly be moral, and keep due metes and bounds, which I dearly love, and allow the most to the will of man; but I have set my heart on honesty in this chapter, and I can see nothing at last, in success or failure, than more or less of vital force supplied from the Eternal. The results of life are uncalculated and uncalculable. The years teach much which the days never know.

93

Faced with the impossibility of reducing life to calculation, the ancients "exalted Chance into a divinity." But in spite of the seeming randomness of existence, there's a deeper unity or underlying reality. "Underneath the inharmonious and trivial particulars, is a musical perfection, the Ideal journeying always with us, the heaven without rent or seam." We experience it in contemplation and in conversation with profound minds: "By persisting to read or to think, this region gives further sign of itself, as it were in flashes of light, in sudden discoveries of its profound beauty and repose, as if the clouds that covered it parted at intervals, and showed the approaching traveller the inland mountains, with the tranquil eternal meadows spread at their base, whereon flocks graze, and shepherds pipe and dance."

In passing from surprise to reality, Emerson reaffirms the mysticism of his earlier essays, which stress the importance of insight and ecstasy. In a passage that might have come from "The Over-Soul," Emerson writes that

> every insight from this realm of thought is felt as initial, and promises a sequel. I do not make it; I arrive there, and behold what was there already. . . . I clap my hands in infantine joy and amazement, before the first opening to me of this august magnificence, old with the love and homage of innumerable ages, young with the life of life, the sunbright Mecca of the desert. And what a future it opens! I feel a new heart beating with the love of the new beauty. I am ready to die out of nature, and be born again into this new yet unapproachable America I have found in the West.

Behind and beneath our experience of mood fluctuations, "there is that in us which changes not and which ranks all sensations and states of mind." Our consciousness enables us to discern various levels of reality, from the "first cause" to the "flesh of [the] body." Like the oversoul (which, in essence, it is), our own consciousness is part and parcel of the consciousness of the world. Consciousness is of one primal and unbounded "substance," called by many names, including Fortune, Muse, Holy Ghost, Love, and Thought.

Emerson seems to prefer the metaphor offered by the Chinese philosopher Mencius: vast-flowing vigor. In Mencius's words, "This vigor is supremely great, and in the highest degree unbending.

94

Nourish it correctly and do it no injury, and it will fill up the vacancy between heaven and earth. This vigor accords with and assists justice and reason, and leaves no hunger." In Western culture we have given this generalization the name *Being*. This is as far as the limitations of language will allow us to go. But we must understand that the word represents not a wall, but a doorway, or what Emerson refers to as "interminable oceans." Being is not a static entity, but a source of great possibilities, as suggested by Mencius's phrase vast-flowing vigor.

This notion of a vast potential at the heart of things is what leads to the "universal impulse to believe." There's always the possibility of some new, more complete and inclusive expression of the meaning of life. Every such statement must include "the skepticisms as well as the faiths of society." Skepticism is the necessary limitation of "the affirmative statement," and "the new philosophy" must incorporate such limitations and draw a new circle of affirmations around them.

The limitation of consciousness, if there is one, is that it involves an awareness of self, or self-consciousness. In Emerson's view, this is "the discovery we have made, that we exist." It's equivalent to the notion of the Fall of Man, a recognition of human limitation and fallibility. "We have learned," Emerson says, "that we do not see directly, but mediately, and that we have no means of correcting these colored and distorting lenses which we are, or of computing the amount of their errors."

This Fall involves an inherent subjectiveness in all our perceptions. Because we are rooted in our own self-consciousness, we can't know for certain whether the world exists apart from our imagination of it. And so the last of Emerson's "lords of life" is Subjectiveness. "Perhaps these subject-lenses have a creative power; perhaps there are no objects." We once assumed the world had an objective reality; now we aren't so sure. We forget that "it is the eye that makes the horizon" and that our subjectivity affects how we see things. Human beings are so locked in their subjectivity that only their surfaces touch. They believe in themselves as they do not believe in others. As Emerson says, "Thus inevitably does the universe wear our color, and every object fall successively into the subject itself. . . . As I am, so I see; use what language we will, we can never say anything but what we are. . . ." We are like kittens chasing our own tails: "If you could look with her eyes, you might see her surrounded with hundreds of figures performing complex dramas, with tragic and comic issues, long conversations, many characters, many ups and downs of fate,— and meantime it is only puss and her tail."

In a kind of Nietzschean acceptance of our own limitations, Emerson says we must rely on the virtue of self-trust. It may be unfortunate that our perceptions are inherently subjective, but that's the way it is. "And yet is the God the native of these bleak rocks." We must embrace our situation. "The life of truth is cold, and so far mournful; but it is not the slave of tears, contritions, and perturbations." In the end we must rely on ourselves, focused on our aim and free from the distractions of others.

These, then, are the lords of life, "threads on the loom of time." Emerson doesn't propose to give them any necessary order, only to name them and acknowledge their place in human experience. Nor does he claim any completeness in his account of them. "I am a fragment," he says, "and this is a fragment of me." He's "too young yet . . . to compile a code." At the same time, by his own reckoning, "I am not the novice I was fourteen, nor yet seven years ago." What is the fruit of his experience? "I find a private fruit sufficient. This is a fruit,— that I should not ask for a rash effect from meditations, counsels and the hiving of truths." Emerson is a humble seeker: "All I know is reception; I am and I have: but I do not get, and when I have fancied I had gotten anything, I found I did not. I worship with wonder the great Fortune."

So what are we left with? Emerson comes down on the side of the visionary as opposed to those who hanker "after an overt or practical effect," but his vision is tempered by experience. Idealists often make themselves ridiculous trying to realize their "world of thought." Nevertheless, he suggests that the ideal world, practically and pragmatically conceived, is the one worth striving for. "Patience and patience, we shall win at the last," he says. A good deal of our life is spent eating and sleeping and earning a living. Only in moments do we "entertain a hope and an insight which becomes the light of our life." All our daily activities, which consume so much of our time, are quickly forgotten because they are so routine, "but in the solitude to which every man is always returning, he has a sanity and revelations, which in his passage into new worlds he will carry with him."

"Experience" ends on a positive note, but not with the confident optimism of Emerson's earlier essays. In the middle years of his life, Emerson finds himself humbled and humanized, but not defeated or disillusioned by experience. The conclusion of the essay gives us a picture of one who has suffered much—the death of a wife, brothers, and a young son—and yet carries on, deeply affected, to be sure, but undaunted. His final words of "Experience" are:

> Never mind the ridicule, never mind the defeat; up again, old heart!
> ... there is victory yet for all justice; and the true romance which the world exists to realize, will be the transformation of genius into practical power.

⑥

You know of the disease in Central Africa called sleeping sickness. . . . There also exists a sleeping sickness of the soul. Its most dangerous aspect is that one is unaware of its coming. That is why you have to be careful. As soon as you notice the slightest sign of indifference, the moment you become aware of the loss of a certain seriousness, of longing, of enthusiasm and zest, take it as a warning. You should realize your soul suffers if you live superficially.

—Albert Schweitzer, "Waking the Sleeping Soul"

I've come to believe, through many years of reading and thinking about this issue, that the soul is really very broad, much broader than we tend to think. It encompasses not just the higher or transcendent level of consciousness, the realm that we traditionally call spirit, but also what we might refer to as the lower level of consciousness—the soul in ordinary experience, the soul in everyday life.

The higher level has to do with developing an overview or philosophy of life, a sense of moral conviction, an idea of what the world is all about and our place in it. These concerns have long been highly valued and addressed through worship, prayer, and other traditional forms of spirituality.

*I have devoted most of my writing and teaching to emphasizing
the lower part of the soul, not because I believe the higher part is
unimportant—it is indeed important—but because the lower aspect
has been so neglected. What I mean by this lower level is the value of
living one's day-to-day life with attention to essential everyday qualities such as beauty, intimacy, community, [and] imagination. . . .
We need to rediscover this awareness. . . . We don't need to look up
to the sky, to some infinite emptiness, in order to find the sacred. That
search has its place, but a sense of the infinite is only part of a much
fuller spirituality that can encompass ordinary experience as well.*

—Thomas Moore, "Embracing the Everyday"

Questions for Personal Reflection and Group Discussion

- Have you ever felt trapped in the mundane aspects of your life
  and without the energy to change your situation?

- How would you describe your temperament? Do you feel determined by it?

- How do you fill your hours? Are you satisfied that you use them
  well?

- What are some "small mercies" that you are thankful for? How
  do you express your gratitude?

- What are some things that surprised you out of your compla-
  cency? Do you prefer life to be predictable or unpredictable?

- What, if anything, remains the same for you though everything
  else changes? How do you characterize the nature of ultimate
  reality?

- What is the place of doubt and skepticism in your own religious
  viewpoint?

- What is the fruit of your own experience of life? How have you grown wise with the years? Do you find yourself optimistic or pessimistic about life?

FATE

The day of days, the great day of the feast of life, is that in which the inward eye opens to the Unity in things, to the omnipresence of law:—sees that what is must be and ought to be, or is the best. This beatitude dips from on high down on us, and we see. It is not in us so much as we are in it. If the air come to our lungs, we breathe and live; if not, we die. If the light come to our eyes, we see; else not. And if truth come to our mind, we suddenly expand to its dimensions, as if we grew to worlds. We are as lawgivers; we speak for Nature; we prophesy and divine.

The subject of fate was on Emerson's mind for a long time. His first lecture on the topic was in 1851, almost ten years before this essay appeared in *Conduct of Life* (1860). He also devoted an entire notebook to the subject. Clearly, fate represented a spiritual issue that Emerson felt he needed to address. Why was he so concerned about this issue? Largely because he had asserted the infinitude of the self-reliant individual. It was also hard to ignore the fact that human beings are subject to tragedy and suffering and that social problems, such as slavery, seem intractable. These seemed to negate Emerson's assertions concerning the unlimited nature of human potential.

Emerson says that the essay is in response to a series of discussions he noticed in Boston and elsewhere on the "Spirit of the Times." For Emerson the topic resolves itself into the "practical question of the conduct of life." The times we live in, whether the tumultuous years leading up to the Civil War, as in Emerson's case, or the first decade of the twenty-first century, represent a confluence of larger forces and prevailing ideas that is too great to comprehend or resolve. "We are incompetent to solve the times," he says; the only question that matters is, "How shall I live?"

The dilemma that we face in every era is how to reconcile freedom and fate. There are always those forces that seem inexorable and beyond our control. At the same time, there's the equally unmistakable fact that, as human beings, we possess agency and free will. "If we must accept Fate," Emerson says, "we are not less compelled to affirm liberty, the significance of the individual, the grandeur of duty, the power of character." If the one is true, so is the other. How to reconcile them is the question.

Emerson won't entertain a facile solution of the problem. Fate seems to preclude freedom. But if liberty is real, there must be some limitation to necessity. We each must resolve this dilemma for ourselves by carefully and honestly examining one by one "the leading topics which belong to our scheme of human life." But let's face it, Emerson says, Americans have a penchant for superficiality. Other people and other nations have confronted the terrors of life by adopting a fatalistic attitude. In the case of the Greeks, the Muslims, the Hindus, even the Calvinists, a belief in fate gave them dignity and strength. The wise have ever felt "that there is something which cannot be talked or voted away—a strap or belt which girds the world."

If "the great immense mind of Jove is not to be transgressed," neither is nature. In spite of our belief in providence, "Nature is no sentimentalist,—does not cosset or pamper us. We must see that the world is rough and surly, and will not mind drowning a man or a woman, but swallows your ship like a grain of dust." Diseases, the elements, fortune, and the forces of nature are no respecters of persons:

The way of Providence is a little rude. The habit of snake and spider, the snap of the tiger and other leapers and bloody jumpers, the crackle of the bones of his prey in the coil of the anaconda,—these are in the system, and our habits are like theirs.

We dine in the shadow of the slaughterhouse. The planet is beset by earthquakes and volcanoes. Emerson cites a litany of natural disasters that have lead to large-scale loss of human life. We can't deny the indiscriminate destructiveness of nature. "Providence has a wild, rough, incalculable road to its end," Emerson insists, "and it is of no use to try to whitewash its huge, mixed instrumentalities, or to dress up that terrific benefactor in a clean shirt and white neckcloth of a student in divinity."

We are even more determined by heredity and upbringing. We can't escape from our ancestry and our genetic makeup. We are born with certain qualities. Emerson writes, "All the privilege and all the legislation in the world cannot meddle or help to make a poet or prince" of us. We are so influenced by forces and factors beyond our control that religions and philosophies have postulated notions such as *karma*, destiny, and predestination to account for their effects.

Life is power, infinitely varied and full of possibilities. But life has its limitations. "Once we thought positive power was all," Emerson notes. "Now we learn, that negative power, or circumstance, is half." Nature is tyrannous as well as beneficial. In the course of evolution we see that there's no turning back. The advance of civilization favors one group and then another. The science of statistics makes everything a matter of fixed calculation. The notions of novelty and invention are undermined by their predictability. Even disease and death are subject to the mathematics of actuarial tables.

We can not escape the conclusion that we are determined by circumstances beyond our control. Emerson concludes, "The force with which we resist these torrents of tendency looks so ridiculously inadequate, that it amounts to little more than a criticism or a protest made by a minority of one, under compulsion of millions." Moreover, our view of life can have no validity unless it admits such troublesome facts. It must be admitted that "a man's power is hooped in by a necessity, which, by many experiments, he touches on every side, until he learns its arc."

Fate is known to us as limitation. Whether we depict it in terms of blind forces or religious doctrines, we are bound, like Fenris in Norse mythology, by the fetters of necessity. Nothing can escape it. Fate is the great leveler, bringing down the high, lifting up the low, impossible even for God to resist for long. Emerson acknowledges that "Fate is immense," but he also writes, "so is power, which is the other fact in the dual world, immense."

If Fate limits power, power thwarts fate. Fate may be equated with natural history, but, as Emerson writes,

> Man is not order of nature, sack and sack, belly and members, link in a chain, nor any ignominious baggage; but a stupendous antagonism, a dragging together of the poles of the Universe. He betrays his relation to what is below him. . . . But the lightening which explodes and fashions planets, maker of planets and suns, is in him.

If there's matter, there's also mind; if there's fate, there's also freedom. We can no more deny free will than we can ignore necessity. We have the ability to choose and to act. "Intellect annuls Fate," Emerson concludes. Insofar as we think, we are free.

To dwell on our limitations, to try to read our destiny in the stars or in tea leaves, is to invite the evils we fear. We should not blame fate for our circumstances or use it as an excuse. Rather, an acknowledgment of limitation should empty us of our conceits and "teach a fatal courage." If fate is powerful, so are human beings, for they are part of it and can confront fate with fate. They offer resistance to the forces of entropy and annihilation.

But Emerson does not envision a standoff between fate and freedom, as though the two cancel each other out. In the end freedom vanquishes fate by means of "the noble creative forces," the first of which is thought. By *thought*, Emerson doesn't mean mere mental activity, but vision or insight that liberates us from servitude to necessity. In such moments we see ourselves as part and parcel of the universe. We assert that what's true of the universe is true of us. We are made strong by its strength, immortal by its timelessness.

Insight is liberating, and the knowledge that comes from insight is a form of power. Those who see through the design preside over it, "and must will that which must be." Emerson cites a certain divine inevitability, "a permanent westerly current," that carries us and everything else along with it: "A breath of will blows eternally through the universe of souls in the direction of the Right and Necessary. It is the air which all intellects inhale and exhale, and it is the wind which blows the worlds into order and orbit."

The second of the "noble creative forces" is the moral sentiment, or conscience. We lend our weight to what we believe to be true. We wish to see the truth prevail. The feeling that we are in league with "the universal force" gives us great strength. As Emerson says, "the pure sympathy with universal ends is an infinite force, and cannot be bribed or bent. Whoever has had experience of the moral sentiment cannot choose but believe in unlimited power." Courage and heroism in the face of apparently insurmountable obstacles give the lie to a fatalistic approach to human history.

According to Emerson, thought and sentiment coalesce in will. Neither suffices by itself. "Perception is cold, and goodness dies in wishes." A fusion of the two is necessary to generate will, without which there can be no driving force. "The one serious and formidable thing in nature is a will," he insists. For want of it, society languishes and looks to "saviours and religions."

Most people compartmentalize power and fate, believing they have free will in their immediate relations with others, "in social circles, in letters, in art, in love, in religion." But in the world of nature, politics, and trade "they believe a malignant energy rules." Emerson refuses to allow for a dualism of fate and freedom. As far as he's concerned, "Fate . . . is a name for facts not yet passed under the fire of thought; for causes which are unpenetrated."

Fate is constrained by thought: "every jet of chaos which threatens to exterminate us is convertible by intellect into wholesome force." Water may drown a ship or a sailor, but "trim your bark" or learn to swim and you have mastered this elemental force. We are not helpless in the face of fate. Diseases may kill thousands, but we can destroy the disease. Steam may be dangerous, but it can be harnessed. And so it is with politics. Human unrest may find channels of power and energy through the democratic process.

We don't like to think we are constrained by fate. If we can turn it to our advantage, so much the better. "If Fate is ore and quarry, if evil is good in the making, if limitation is power that shall be, if calamities, oppositions, and weights are wings and means,—we are reconciled." The tendency of the universe is progressive. "The direction of the whole and of the parts is toward benefit." Behind us is fate that has been meliorated; before us are human freedom and a better world. Therefore, according to Emerson, "Liberation of the will from the sheaths and clogs of organization which [it] has outgrown, is the end and aim of this world."

Since everything is interconnected, it's hard to know where fate leaves off and freedom begins. "This knot of nature is so well tied, that nobody was ever cunning enough to find the two ends." Suffice it to say that a balance exists between them such that everything—inanimate as well as animate—seems suited to its environment: eyes in light, feet on land, wings in air, and so on, "each creature where it was meant to be, with a mutual fitness." A certain kind of intelligence is at work in the interplay of these natural forces, which becomes self-directing "as soon as there is life."

This applies to the human world as well, in the relationship between people and events. We are suited to our fortunes, which are the fruit of our character. "The pleasure of life," Emerson asserts, "is according to the man that lives it, and not according to the work or the place. Life is an ecstasy." Each creature, from slug to human being, "puts forth from itself its own condition and sphere." Indeed, all of history is the action and reaction of nature and thought: "two boys pushing each other on the curb-stone of the pavement. Everything is pusher or pushed: and matter and mind are in perpetual tilt and balance, so."

This intricate interaction accounts for the "wonderful constancy in the design this vagabond life admits." The key to the solution of the mysteries of the human condition and "the old knots" of fate and freedom lies in the propounding of "the double consciousness." Our life oscillates between outside forces and inner states of being, or nature and thought. When it seems that we're victims of fate, we need "to rally on [our] relation to the Universe, which our ruin benefits."

These two opposites comprise a "Blessed Unity" that is ultimately providential. This unity "holds nature and souls in perfect solution, and compels every atom to serve an universal end." Beyond the wonder of the snowflake and the glory of the stars, there's the awe and reverence that are awakened "when the indwelling necessity plants the rose of beauty on the brow of chaos, and discloses the central intention of Nature to be harmony and joy."

"Let us build alters to the Beautiful Necessity," Emerson says. Human freedom is not license to alter the order of things. "If, in the least particular, one could derange the order of nature,—who would accept the gift of life?" Everything is made of one piece: "plaintiff and defendant, friend and enemy, animal and planet, food and eater, are of one kind." We should not fear nature. There's no danger that we are not equipped to face. There are no contingencies or exceptions. Law rules throughout the universe. Law, in Emerson's words, "is not intelligent but intelligence,—not personal nor impersonal,—it disdains words and passes understanding; it dissolves persons; it vivifies nature; yet solicits the pure in heart to draw on all its omnipotence."

Freedom is a fact of experience not to be denied. But it's not the total freedom Emerson had envisioned and espoused in his earlier essays. Our freedom, like everything else in life, is limited and partial. Although our freedom is conditional and contingent, it's encompassed by a providential view of the natural order of things.

The first step to the knowledge of the wonder and mystery of life is the recognition of the monstrous nature of the earthly realm as well as its glory, the realization that this is just how it is and that it cannot and will not be changed. Those who think they know—and their name is legion—how the universe could have been had they created it, without pain, without sorrow, without time, without death, are unfit for illumination.

So if you really want to help this world, what you will have to teach is how to live in it. And that no one can do who has not themselves

107

learned how to live in the joyful sorrow and the sorrowful joy of the
knowledge of life as it is.
—Joseph Campbell, quoted in Jack Kornfield, ed.,
The Art of Forgiveness, Lovingkindness, and Peace

It is reassuring to feel we are not alone in a hostile universe, but rather
we are allied with a creative power which seeks us out, which
strengthens and inspires us, which needs our eyes and ears and tongues.
We are not puppets tugged by invisible strings, but free players in the
drama of Creation. We learn the script as we go, and we also help to
compose it, we and all our fellow beings. In our search for knowledge
and our struggle for expression we are carrying on the Creator's work,
and in that work we are aided by the Way of things. To recognize the
possibility of such aid is to believe in grace. So we are justified in feeling
not merely human optimism, based on our own intelligence and skills,
but cosmic optimism, based on the nature of reality.
—Scott Russell Sanders, *Hunting for Hope*

Questions for Personal Reflection and Group Discussion

- Emerson felt that in the face of conditions and circumstances beyond our control, the only question that matters is, "How shall I live?" How do you answer this question for yourself?

- How do you reconcile yourself to those forces, natural and otherwise, that threaten human life and liberty? What is your take on fate? Do you resist or acquiesce?

- The picture Emerson paints of nature in "Fate" seems different from the more benign view he had in his earlier essays. Do you see any inconsistency or contradiction here? Can nature be both providential and indifferent?

- To what extent do you feel that you are determined by your temperament, heredity, and upbringing?

- Emerson feels that nothing is more powerful than the will hitched to an ideal. Do you agree? Can you cite any evidence?

- Is the tendency of the universe progressive and providential? Why or why not?

- Emerson insists that "life is an ecstasy." What do you suppose he means by this? Do you find it to be true in your own life? What evidence can you point to?

WORSHIP

There is a principle which is the basis of things, which all speech aims to say, and all action to evolve, a simple, quiet, undescribed, undescribable presence, dwelling very peacefully in us, our rightful lord: we are not to do, but to let do; not to work, but to be worked upon; and to this homage there is a consent of all thoughtful and just men in all ages and conditions. To this sentiment belong vast and sudden enlargements of power. 'Tis remarkable that our faith in ecstasy consists with total inexperience of it. It is the order of the world to educate with accuracy the senses and the understanding; and the enginery at work to draw out these powers in priority, no doubt, has its office. But we are never without a hint that these powers are mediate and servile, and that we are one day to deal with real being,—essences with essences.

In 1851 Emerson began a series of lectures that were collected and published in 1860 as *The Conduct of Life*. Among them was "Worship," written in 1858. What does it mean to be moral? Can we be moral without being religious in the traditional sense? In what way is work a spiritual issue? These are some of the questions posed in "Worship."

Here Emerson returns to the theme of religion, which he first examined in his celebrated address to the students at Harvard

Divinity School in 1838. In that speech he challenged religious formalism. Twenty years later, he contends that skepticism has thoroughly discredited religious doctrines and institutions, but not the innate spiritual or moral sentiment that gives rise to religions in the first place. For Emerson, the spiritual and the moral are essentially synonymous. If he emphasized the spiritual, that is, the mystical, intuitive nature of religion in the "Divinity School Address," in "Worship" he emphasizes the moral quality of religion—its ethical, pragmatic, practical side and its application to everyday life.

Although he doesn't mention the *Bhagavad Gita*, Emerson's thinking was greatly influenced by this Hindu classic, which he read with increasing interest and admiration during the 1840s and 1850s. He was particularly drawn to the notion that we must perform the work we are meant to do without regard to rewards. Moreover, in Emerson's view, when acts are done in accordance with the natural order of things, they may be said to be moral. This appears to be the sense in which he uses the word in this essay.

Emerson begins by telling of friends' complaints that other lectures collected in *The Conduct of Life* were too concerned with temporal issues, such as fate, power, and wealth, the ambiguities of which stimulated doubt and undermined belief. But Emerson thinks a "good soul" has nothing to fear from skepticism. "A just thinker will allow full swing to his skepticism," he says. "I dip my pen into the blackest ink, because I am not afraid of falling into my inkpot."

We may give skepticism the widest range, Emerson insists, knowing that faith is innate and natural. "We are born believing," he says. "A man bears beliefs, as a tree bears apples. A self-poise belongs to every particle; and a rectitude to every mind, and is the Nemesis and protector of every society." In other words, we may think we wouldn't be moral without a church or a creed, but that is not the case. In fact, faith adheres to the soul and survives in spite of the eclipse of religions and theologians. Indeed, "God builds his temple in the heart on the ruins of churches and religions."

Earlier lectures dealt with particular aspects of self-culture, which in its fullest sense may be described as religion or worship. Emerson felt that religion often reflects the baser motives of society. We are fortunate that "souls out of time, extraordinary, prophetic, are born, who are rather related to the system of the world than to their particular age and locality." These prophets and visionaries announce absolute truths, which are, unfortunately, often distorted.

Emerson felt that he lived in a transitional period in which the traditional religions seemed to have spent their force and lost their moral and intellectual credibility. Their followers had succumbed to doubt and materialism. Emerson writes that there is "no bond, no fellow-feeling, no enthusiasm. These are not men, but hungers, thirsts, fevers, and appetites walking. How is it people manage to live on,—so aimless as they are?" Their faith is in machines and material goods, not in "divine causes." For creeds, they have substituted superstition and séances. What better evidence of the decline of religion than the toleration of slavery and "the base rate at which the highest mental and moral gifts are held?"

The general lack of virtue and character is further evidence. "It is believed by well-dressed proprietors that there is no more virtue than they possess; that the solid proportion of society exist for the arts of comfort; that life is an affair to put somewhat between the upper and lower mandibles." People are cynical and suspicious of the motives of others. Even the "well-disposed, good sort of people" are compromised by their clinging to the past.

This lack of faith is so prevalent that people are inclined to view it as normative. But, as Emerson says, "the multitude of the sick shall not make us deny the existence of health." In spite of the infidelity of so many, to say that there is no basis for religion is "like saying in rainy weather, there is no sun, when at that moment we are witnessing one of his superlative effects." Behind or beneath the distortions of religion exists the possibility of living a spiritual life, if we will but wait for the clouds to clear.

We must free ourselves from the religious systems of the past. Faith itself suffers from conformity. "Religion must always be a crab fruit," Emerson says, "it cannot be grafted and keep its wild beauty." Nor can it be saved by any modification of creeds or practices. The only cure for "false theology" is living a moral and spiritual life, based on an intuitive perception of the laws that "pervade and govern" the universe, omnipresent in every atom in nature. When we learn to act out of an intuition of moral laws and not out of a fear of being cheated or caught, then all goes well. We have changed our "market-cart into a chariot of the sun."

Worship functions as the source of intellect. By intellect Emerson means thought or insight into what he terms the Universal Mind, rather than reasoning or analysis. "All the great ages have been ages of belief," times when "the human soul was in earnest, and had fixed its thoughts on spiritual verities." Genius, the essence of who we are, derives from an apprehension of the moral sentiment. Those who are able to cultivate this sentiment "are nearer to the secret of God than others; are bathed by sweeter waters; they hear notices, they see visions, where others are vacant." Intellect and morals are interdependent, although Emerson indicates that character, which is the measure of our moral sensibility, declines with the "acceptance of the lucrative standard." Thus morality would appear to have priority over the intellect.

Human beings have learned to weigh and measure the sun. They should also discover the laws of the moral universe. Religion or worship is the attitude of those who have insight into these laws and see that "the nature of things works for truth and right forever." There is cause and effect in the moral universe as well as in the physical world. In Emerson's words:

> A man does not see, that, as he eats, so he thinks; as he deals, so he is, and so he appears; . . . that fortunes are not exceptions but fruit; that relation and connection are not somewhere and sometimes, but everywhere and always; no miscellany, no exemption, no anomaly,— but method, and an even web; and what comes out, that was put in. As we are, so we do; and as we do, so is it done to us; we are the builders of our fortunes.

These laws are operative in nature and the human mind. They form the basis of what we experience as the moral sentiment. They hold sway everywhere. Emerson contends "that the dice are loaded; that the colors are fast, because they are the native colors of the fleece; that the globe is a battery, because every atom is a magnet; and that the police and sincerity of the universe are secured by God's delegating his divinity to every particle; that there is no room for hypocrisy, no margin for choice."

These are universal laws. It doesn't matter where we go, the truth will out because we can't hide any secret. If we spend for show, it will so appear. "There is no privacy that cannot be penetrated," Emerson insists. "No secret can be kept in the civilized world. Society is a masked ball, where every one hides his real character, and reveals it by hiding." Our character is always shown for what it is. We are known by our work and by our actions. Character affects not only how the world sees us but also how we view the world. "That only which we have within, can we see without," Emerson notes. "If we meet no gods, it is because we harbor none. If there is grandeur in you, you will find grandeur in porters and sweeps."

The qualities that we value in human life—love, humility, and faith—are in the very atoms. Because we are part and parcel of a moral universe, we are "equal to every event" that transpires. We are protected from danger so long as our actions are consistent with the life that nature has laid out for us. Our task, as we understand it, is our life-preserver. "The conviction that [our] work is dear to God and cannot be spared, defends [us]." There is thus a moral quality to our work. When we perform it, the weight of the world is on our side.

The kind of morality Emerson insists upon is different from the virtue that is praised by society and promoted by religion. He writes, "The highest virtue is always against the law." We do what we do because it's right for us, not because of praise or esteem. Greatness is not a matter of calculation, but of inspiration, of following one's calling. When the soul is "well employed," it doesn't worry about immortality. "Immortality will come to such as are fit for it," Emerson insists, "and he who would be a great soul in the future, must be a great soul now."

Religion discourages us from our task because it finds us unworthy. But the truth of the matter is that we are suited to our work, and it's essential that we do it. In Emerson's view, "The weight of the Universe is pressed down on the shoulders of each moral agent to hold him to his task. The only path of escape known in all the worlds of God is performance. You must do your work, before you shall be released." This is a spiritual truth written into law by "the government of the universe" and may be summarized this way:

The last lesson of life, the choral song which rises from all elements and all angels, is a voluntary obedience, a necessitated freedom. Man is made of the same atoms as the world is, he shares the same impressions, predispositions and destiny. When his mind is illuminated, when his heart is kind, he throws himself joyfully into the sublime order, and does, with knowledge, what the stones do by structure.

Therefore, a religion that "is to guide and fulfil the present and coming ages," must be intellectual," by which Emerson means cognizant of the "moral science" he has aimed to describe. A new church founded on ethical law may lack the trappings of traditional religion, "but it will have heaven and earth for its beams and rafters." Its self-reliant adherents will be motivated by the pursuit of "high causes" rather than the approval of others.

The ethical problem is the problem of finding a foundation in thought for the fundamental principle of morality. What is the common element of good in the manifold kinds of good which we encounter in our experience? Does such a general notion of good really exist?

If so, then what is its essential nature, and to what extent is it real and necessary for me? What power does it possess over my opinions and actions? What is the position it brings me with regard to the world?

Thought, therefore, must direct its attention to this fundamental moral principle. The mere setting up of lists of virtues and vices is like vamping on the keyboard and calling the ensuing noise music.
—Albert Schweitzer, *Civilization and Ethics*

The state of our whole life is estrangement from others and ourselves, because we are estranged from the Ground of our being, because we are estranged from the origin and aim of our life. And we do not know where we have come from, or where we are going. We are separated from the mystery, the depth, and the greatness of our existence. We hear the voice of that depth; but our ears are closed.
—Paul Tillich, "You Are Accepted"

Questions for Personal Reflection and Group Discussion

- Emerson believes that human beings are "born believing," that is to say, inherently religious. Do you agree? Do you consider yourself a religious person?

- Dostoyevsky believed that without God everything is permissible. Emerson insists that humans are innately moral and that morality does not depend upon churches or creeds. Who do you think is right? Can people be moral without religion?

- Emerson argues that traditional religions have spent their force and lost their intellectual and moral credibility. More than 150 years later, they are still very much with us. Was Emerson wrong?

- Emerson clearly makes a distinction between religion and spirituality. Is this a distinction that is helpful to you?

- How can religion keep its "wild beauty"? Must it always sanction conformity?

- How do you cultivate the moral sense in yourself? How do you hone your own character? To what extent does your character shape the world that you see?

- "The highest virtue is always against the law," Emerson says. What do you suppose he means by this?

- Emerson admonishes us to discern and adhere to the "sublime order" of things, to engage in a voluntary obedience to divine providence. This, he suggests, is what it means to worship or be worshipful. Does this make sense to you? Would you agree?

ILLUSIONS

From day to day the capital facts of human life are hidden from our eyes. Suddenly the mist rolls up, and reveals them, and we think how much good time is gone, that might have been saved, had any hint of these things been shown. A sudden rise in the road shows us the system of mountains, and all the summits, which have been just as near us all the year, but quite out of mind.

The essays in *The Conduct of Life* primarily have to do with issues of human agency and ethical action. Each attempts to answer the question first posed in "Fate," namely, "How shall I live?" In "Illusions" the question might be put as follows: Given the shifting sands of perception and the illusions of everyday life, is there a moral ground for human action?

Emerson must have had Plato's allegory of the cave from *The Republic* in mind when he wrote of his visit to Kentucky's Mammoth Cave in 1850. In Plato's allegory the observer views shadows on the wall of a cave, mistaking them for the real world rather than for the illusions they are. The source of these shadows, namely the light, comes from outside the cave.

Deep inside Mammoth Cave the lamps were extinguished and the visitors were treated to what appeared to be a show of stars with "a flaming comet among them." The illusion reminded Emerson of similar experiences, demonstrating the extent to which imagination embellishes our experience, contributing to our appreciation of "sunset glories, rainbows, and northern lights."

The imagination also affects our experience of pleasure and pain. We are mistaken, Emerson says, if we believe that "the circumstance gives the joy which we give to the circumstance." If life is sweet, it's because we attribute a certain pleasure to the activities we engage in. We cherish our illusions, often preferring them to reality. "We live by our imaginations, by our admirations, by our sentiments," he observes. "The child walks amid heaps of illusions, which he does not like to have disturbed."

We fantasize that we live better lives than we actually do. Society is a carnival and does not like to be unmasked. To some extent, we are all victims of illusion, "led by one bawble or another." The power of the gods and goddesses of illusion is stronger than that of the other gods. They weave their spell around us, leaving us confused:

> All is riddle, and the key to a riddle is another riddle. There are as many pillows of illusion as flakes in a snow-storm. We wake from one dream into another dream. The toys, to be sure, are various, and are graduated in refinement to the quality of the dupe. . . . But everybody is drugged with his own frenzy, and the pageant marches at all hours, with music and banner and badge.

Not everyone is taken in. A few see that the emperor has no clothes, but "the enchantments are laid on very thick." They affect our circumstances and our relationships. Even the scholar in his library is susceptible. However, we admire people who can "lift a corner of the curtain" to reveal what's behind it. It helps to know that there are gradations in "the phantasms," from the lowest of masks to the most subtle and beautiful. What if we discover that the importance we attach to things radiates from ourselves and "that the sun borrows his beams"? Once we believed in magic. Now it has been dispelled, along with "all vestige of theism and beliefs." From deceptions of the senses to illusions of the intellect, all experience is subject to the workings of the imagination, so much so that we delude ourselves as to our own role in it.

Science treats time and space as forms of thought and the material world as hypothetical. Every generalization yields to a larger one. Our estimates of things are loose and floating. "We must work and affirm," Emerson says, "but we have no guess of the value of what we say or do." The things that seem trivial to us are actually of the greatest significance. In Emerson's view, "if we weave a yard of tape in all humility, and as well as we can, long hereafter we shall see it was no cotton tape at all, but some galaxy which we braided, and that the threads were Time and Nature."

If we can't predict the order of the variable winds, "how can we penetrate the law of our shifting moods and susceptibility"? The firmament that once existed is gone and with it the stars that might have signaled our destiny. We seem to be adrift. Yet we need not fear. Life may be a succession of dreams, but the "visions of good men are good." It's only the undisciplined will that is "whipped with bad thoughts and bad fortunes."

"In this kingdom of illusions we grope eagerly for stays and foundations," Emerson observes. These prove to be quite simple and personal really: honesty and truth—with ourselves and others—are what we must rely on. "Speak as you think, be what you are, pay your debts of all kinds." Cheats live for appearances, "it is what we really are that avails with friends, with strangers, and with fate or fortune." In other words, Emersonian self-reliance is the key to finding one's way in a world clouded by appearance and cluttered with triviality.

We think having riches and avoiding poverty means a great deal, but the Native Americans do not think the white man, "with his brow of care, always toiling, afraid of heat and cold, and keeping within doors," has any advantage over them. "The permanent interest of every man, is never to be in a false position," Emerson insists, "but to have the weight of Nature to back him in all that he does." Riches and poverty are but a costume; the life of all of humankind is identical. We are all capable of transcending our circumstances and tasting the true quality of existence.

According to the Hindus, variety and separateness are illusory; only the unity of things is real. The waves come and go, but the ocean remains the same. Although the intellect and the will are prey to deception, "the unities of Truth and Right are not broken by the disguise." We don't need to be confused about these. "In a crowded life of many parts and performers, on a stage of nations, or in the obscurest hamlet in Maine or California, the same elements offer the same choices to each new comer, and, according to his election, he fixes his fortune in absolute Nature."

Thus, beneath or behind the world of appearances exists a reality we can be certain of and rely on. "There is no chance, and no anarchy, in the universe," Emerson insists. He concludes the essay with an allegory of his own that, like Plato's, reveals both the discovery of illusion and the affirmation of reality:

> The young mortal enters the hall of the firmament; there he is alone with them alone, they pouring on him benedictions and gifts, and beckoning him up to their thrones. On the instant, and incessantly, fall snow-storms of illusions. He fancies himself in a vast crowd which sways this way and that and whose movement and doings he must obey: he fancies himself poor, orphaned, insignificant. The mad crowd drives hither and thither, now furiously commanding this thing to be done, now that. What is he that he should resist their will, and think or act for himself? Every moment, new changes, and new showers of deceptions, to baffle and distract him. And when, by and by, for an instant, the air clears and the cloud lifts a little, there are the gods still sitting around him on their thrones,—they alone with him alone.

We are all subject to the "snow-storms of illusions," including those delusions that suggest we are isolated and insignificant and incapable of thinking or acting on our own. Occasionally, "the air clears and the cloud lifts a little," revealing that our actual existence is among the gods who pour on us their "benedictions and gifts" and beckon us to live a fuller, richer, deeper life in their presence.

Most people believe the mind to be a mirror, more or less accurately reflecting the world outside of them, not realizing on the contrary that the mind is itself the principle element of creation.
    —Rabindranath Tagore, quoted in Jack Kornfield, ed.,
        The Art of Forgiveness, Lovingkindness, and Peace

Maya comes from the same root as magic. In saying the world is maya, non-dual Hinduism is saying there is something tricky about it. The trick lies in the way the world's materiality and multiplicity pass themselves off as being independently real—real apart from the stance from which we see them—whereas in fact reality is undifferentiated Brahman throughout, even as a rope lying in the dust remains a rope while being mistaken for a snake. Maya is also seductive in the attractiveness in which it presents the world, trapping us within it and leaving us with no desire to journey on.

—Huston Smith, *The World's Religions*

Questions for Personal Reflection and Group Discussion

- To what extent do you believe that one's imagination—including one's fantasies and fears—creates the reality we seem to perceive?

- Emerson claims that we are all victims of illusions and, in many cases, willing victims. Do you agree? What evidence would you cite for believing so?

- What illusions have been dispelled for you? How did you feel as a result of this discovery of illusion?

- Do you believe, as Emerson does, that there's a reality beneath appearances? What are some constants for you in your own experience?

- Emerson insists "there is no chance or anarchy in the universe." Do you agree or disagree?

- What would you say are some of the "benedictions and gifts" you have received from the gods?

Daughters of Time, the hypocritic Days,
Muffled and dumb like barefoot dervishes,
And marching single in an endless file,
Bring diadems and fagots in their hands.
To each they offer gifts after his will,
Bread, kingdoms, stars and sky that holds them all.
I, in my pleached garden, watched the pomp,
Forgot my morning wishes, hastily
Took a few herbs and apples, and the Day
Turned and departed silent. I, too late,
Under her solemn fillet saw the scorn.

"Works and Days" dates from 1857, but did not appear in print until 1870 as one of the twelve chapters of Emerson's last book, *Society and Solitude.* As with several of the essays in this volume, "Works and Days" has the quality of summing up accumulated wisdom on various topics. The title is taken from a work by the Greek poet Hesiod, which consists of moral maxims and precepts on farming and everyday life.

Like most of Emerson's essays, "Works and Days" is prefaced with a poem, in this case, one of his personal favorites. It appears whole or in bits and pieces in various of his writings, including his journals. It expresses a thought that is central to his philosophy of life, that every day the world is laid out for us in this garden that is our home. We are given the precious gift of time to make the most of. But these priceless moments are for this day only. Any that go unused are taken away. In this poem Emerson has forgotten his morning wishes (his hopes and dreams and best intentions) and settles for only a few herbs and apples. He realizes too late that he has made little use of the time he was given.

The nineteenth century, Emerson observes, is the age of tools, of machines. But these instruments are only extensions of ourselves, our limbs and senses. Man is truly the measure of all things. Nevertheless, advances of science and technology are exciting; "so many inventions have been added that life seems almost made over." One after another, these inventions have transformed society on a scale previously unimagined. They have made "day out of night, time out of space, and space out of time." Emerson summarizes these developments:

> Yes, we have a pretty artillery of tools now in our social arrangements: we ride four times as fast as our fathers did; travel, grind, weave, forge, plant, till and excavate better. We have new shoes, gloves, glasses and gimlets; we have the calculus, we have the newspaper, which does its best to make every square acre of land give an account of itself at your breakfast table; we have money, and paper money; we have language,—the finest tool of all, and nearest the mind. Much will have more. Man flatters himself that his command over Nature must increase. Things begin to obey him.

But Emerson is troubled by the incessant demand for such improvements. It's a thirst that can't be quenched. No matter how many centuries of advance have preceded, "the new man always finds himself on the brink of chaos, always in a crisis." When were sensible men and women ever plentiful?

Emerson insists that "we must look deeper for our salvation than to steam, photographs, balloons or astronomy." We have become captives of our own tools. "The weaver becomes a web, the machinist a machine." Once we build a fine house, we have a master and a task for life. For all our mechanical inventions, we have not lightened the day's toil of anyone. What have these done for character or human worth? Are we the better for them? The pace of material power has outstripped moral progress. We have not made a wise investment. We were offered both works and days, and we took only works.

A farmer is said to have wanted the land that joined his own. Napoleon had the same appetite on a larger scale. But even if he had had the world, he would still be a pauper.

He only is rich who owns the day. There is no king, rich man, fairy or demon who possesses such power as that. The days are ever divine. . . . They are of the least pretension and of the greatest capacity of anything that exists. They come and go like muffled and veiled figures, sent from a distant friendly party; but they say nothing, and if we do not use the gifts they bring, they carry them as silently away.

Some days are full of significance. Holidays, for example, are especially memorable—the Fourth of July, Thanksgiving, and Christmas. Likewise school days and college terms when "life was then calendared by moments, [and] threw itself into nervous knots of glittering hours." Even the Sabbath offers "a clean page, which the wise may inscribe with truth." There are days when we feel close to greatness. "There are days which are the carnival of the year. The angels assume flesh, and repeatedly become available." But each day offers its gifts to those who are fit to receive them:

The days are made on a loom whereof the warp and woof are past and future time. They are majestically dressed, as if every god brought a thread to the skyey web. 'Tis pitiful the things by which we are rich or poor,—a matter of coins, coats and carpets, a little more or less stone, or wood, or paint, the fashion of a cloak or hat. . . . But the treasures which Nature spent itself to amass,—the secular, refined, composite anatomy of man . . .; the surrounding plastic natures; the earth with its foods; the intellectual, temperamenting air; the sea with its invitations; the heavens deep with worlds; and the answering brain and nervous structure replying to these; the eye that looketh into the deeps, which again look back to the eye, abyss to abyss;—these, not like . . . coins or carpets, are given immeasurably to all.

Such a miracle is available to each of us, but we do not see it because we are deluded, "coaxed, flattered and duped from morn to eve, from birth to death." Where, Emerson asks, is "the old eye that ever saw through the deception"? If we are caught up in illusion perhaps it's because life is difficult, a "gale of warring elements," and therefore we need to be harnessed to it:

As if . . . it was necessary to bind souls to human life as mariners in a tempest lash themselves to the mast and bulwarks of a ship, and Nature employed certain illusions as her ties and straps,—a rattle, a doll . . . a horse, a gun, for the growing boy; and I will not begin to name those of the youth and adult, for they are numberless. Seldom and slowly the mask falls and the pupil is permitted to see that all is one stuff, cooked and painted under many counterfeit appearances.

Illusion distorts our values. The passing hours with all their "trade, entertainments and gossip" deceive and distract us. Each one is like another, like the news that awaits us when we've been away for a while. We realize "in moments of deeper thought" that we are repeating scenes of the most ancient times, that an "everlasting Now reigns in Nature." That being the case, everything we need is right here, not in the past or somewhere else, in this and not some other hour: "One of the illusions is that the present hour is not the critical, decisive hour. Write it on your heart that every day is the best day in the year. No man has learned anything rightly until he knows that every day is Doomsday."

Since the gods sometimes appear in the guise of beggars, even what seems to be the most trivial hour has everything to offer:

We owe to genius always the same debt, of lifting the curtain from the common, and showing us that divinities are sitting disguised in the seeming gang of gypsies and pedlers. In daily life, what distinguishes the master is the using those materials he has, instead of looking about for what are more renowned, or what others have used well. . . . Do not refuse the employment which the hour brings you, for one more ambitious. The highest heaven of wisdom is alike near from every point, and thou must find it, if at all, by methods native to thyself alone.

Another illusion is that we don't have enough time for our work. When someone remarked to a chief of the Six Nations of New York that he had not enough time, the Native American replied, "Well, I suppose you have all there is." We always have all the time there is. It's up to us to make the best use of it.

A third illusion is that long duration (a year, a decade, a century) is what's truly valuable. An old French saying counters "God works in moments." And Emerson reminds us, "We ask for long life, but 'tis deep life, or grand moments, that signify." The measure of time should be qualitative, not quantitative. "Moments of insight, of fine personal relation, a smile, a glance,—what ample borrowers of eternity they are!" Eternity culminates in the present moment; or as Homer said, "The gods ever give to mortals their apportioned share of reason only on one day."

The measure of a man is "his apprehension of the day." The learned scholar is not one who unearths ancient history, "but who can unfold the theory of this particular Wednesday." The minutes we have are not a way to or from happiness; in fact, they constitute happiness and the only eternity we have. Understood in this way, we are guided from a menial and dependent life to one of riches and fulfillment. We must forego our tendency to analyze and dissect experience:

> . . . life is good only when it is magical and musical, a perfect timing and consent, and when we do not anatomize it. You must treat the days respectfully, you must be a day yourself, and not interrogate it like a college professor. The world is enigmatical . . . and must not be taken literally, but genially. We must be at the top of our condition to understand anything rightly. You must hear the bird's song without attempting to render it into nouns and verbs. Cannot we be a little abstemious and obedient? Cannot we let the morning be?

We should follow the example of native Hawaiians who, in the words of a foreign scholar who visited Emerson in his youth, "delight to play with the surf, coming in on top of the rollers, then swimming out again, and repeat the delicious manoeuvre for hours." The scholar drew the following conclusion:

> Well, human life is made up of such transits. There can be no greatness without abandonment. . . . Just to fill the hour,—that is happiness. Fill my hour, ye gods, so that I shall not say, whilst I have done this, "Behold, also, an hour of my life is gone,"—but rather, "I have lived an hour."

Like the Hawaiian surfers, we should do what we do for the joy of it, rather than from a sense of duty. This rule holds in science as well as literature and the arts.

The quality of the moment and not its duration is what counts. "It is the depth at which we live," Emerson insists, "and not at all the surface extension that imports." Time is but the flitting surface; with "the least acceleration of thought" we pierce through it to eternity and "make life to seem and to be of vast duration." We call it time, but when it is thus penetrated, "it acquires another and a higher name." There are some to whom this comes quite naturally. "This is character," in Emerson's view, "the highest name at which philosophy has arrived."

Character should predominate over talent as days over works. Spiritual progress is a leading upward from talent, or skills, to character:

> And this is the progress of every earnest mind; from the works of man and the activity of the hands to a delight in the faculties which rule them; from a respect to the works to a wise wonder at this mystic element of time in which he is conditioned; from local skills and the economy which reckons the amount of production *per* hour to the finer economy which respects the quality of what is done, and the right we have to the work, or the fidelity with which it flows from ourselves; then to the depth of thought it betrays, looking to its universality, or that its roots are in eternity, not in time. Then it flows from character, that sublime health which values one moment as another, and makes us great in all conditions, and as the only definition we have of freedom and power.

Emerson might as well have been speaking of the twenty-first century as the nineteenth. In our day as much as his, works supersede days, so to speak. And it's just as important for us to achieve a balance between a respect for works and a wise wonder at the mystic element of time in which we live and move and have our being.

⑥

There is only one world, the world pressing against you at this minute. There is only one minute in which you are alive, this minute here and now. The only way to live is by accepting each minute as an unrepeatable miracle.

—Storm Jameson, quoted in Jack Kornfield, ed.
The Art of Forgiveness, Lovingkindness, and Peace

Eternity isn't some later time. Eternity isn't even a long time. Eternity has nothing to do with time. Eternity is that dimension of here and now that all thinking in temporal terms cuts off. And if you don't get it here, you won't get it anywhere . . . the experience of eternity right here and now, in all things . . . is the function of life.

—Joseph Campbell, *The Power of Myth*

Questions for Personal Reflection and Group Discussion

- Emerson characterizes the nineteenth century as an age of tools, of machines. How would you characterize the twenty-first century? Do you see any similarities? Do Emerson's observations still ring true?

- Emerson says we were offered both works and days, but we only took works. Do you agree? Is this still true today, in your view? How have you tried to achieve a balance in your life between works and days?

- Do you feel that you make the best use of the day? How could you make it better?

- How do you feel that your life is made rich?

- What are some of the delusions and deceptions that keep you from appreciating all that the days have to offer?

- What are some of the gods that have approached you in the guise of beggars, gifts that seemed trivial but proved to be valuable?

- In what ways have you tried to let the morning be? What does this mean for you in the way you choose to live your life?

1803	Born May 25 in Boston, Massachusetts.
1804	Father, Rev. William Emerson, dies. Four brothers and sisters die in childhood.
1817–21	Attends Harvard College.
1821–25	Teaches in brother William's school for women.
1825	Enters Harvard Divinity School. Adopts the name Waldo. Studies interrupted by eye troubles.
1826	Approbated to preach by the Middlesex Association of Ministers. Tuberculosis necessitates a trip to the South.
1827	Returns to Boston as an itinerant preacher. Meets Ellen Tucker while preaching in Concord, New Hampshire.
1828	Brother Edward has a breakdown. Becomes engaged to Ellen Tucker.
1829	Becomes associate minister of Boston's Second Church (Unitarian). Although Ellen is ill with tuberculosis, Waldo and Ellen marry.
1831	Ellen dies in February at the age of nineteen. Period of crisis.

1832	Dissatisfied with the ministry as a profession, resigns pulpit. In poor health, sails for Europe.
1833	Visits Italy, France, and England. Meets Samuel Taylor Coleridge, William Wordsworth, and Thomas Carlyle. Returns home.
1834	Lectures in Boston. Moves with mother to the Manse in Concord.
	Brother Edward dies in Puerto Rico.
1835	Lectures again in Boston. Becomes interim minister in East Lexington, Massachusetts.
	Marries Lydia Jackson of Plymouth, Massachusetts. Buys home in Concord.
1836	Brother Charles dies of tuberculosis. Transcendental Club organized.
	First book, *Nature*, published. Son Waldo born.
1837	Delivers "The American Scholar" address at Harvard. Lectures on "Human Culture."
1838	Delivers controversial address at Harvard Divinity School. Forms close friendship with Henry David Thoreau.
1839	Daughter Ellen born.
1840	With Margaret Fuller, publishes first issue of *The Dial*. Declines invitation to join Brook Farm.
1841	First book of *Essays* published. Daughter Edith born.
1842	Son Waldo dies from scarlet fever. Becomes editor of *The Dial*.
	Lectures in New York.
1844	Son Edward born. Delivers antislavery address. Second book of *Essays* published.
1845	Gives Thoreau permission to build a cabin on Emerson property at Walden Pond.

1846	*Poems* published.
1847–48	Takes second trip to Europe. Lectures in England. Meets Charles Dickens; Alfred, Lord Tennyson; and Alexis de Tocqueville.
1849	*Nature, Addresses, and Lectures* published.
1850	*Representative Men* published. Lectures in New England, New York, Philadelphia, Cleveland, and Cincinnati. Death of Margaret Fuller in shipwreck. Begins lecture series on "The Conduct of Life."
1851	Angered by Daniel Webster's defense of the Fugitive Slave Law, advocates disobedience.
1852	Lectures in Boston, St. Louis, Philadelphia, Montreal, and Maine.
1853	Mother dies at the age of eighty-four.
1854	Delivers attack on Fugitive Slave Law in New York.
1855	Delivers antislavery addresses in Boston, New York, and Philadelphia.
1856	*English Traits* published. Helps raise funds for Kansas Relief.
1858	Declares himself an abolitionist.
1860	Lectures in New York State, New England, the Middle West, and Toronto. *Conduct of Life* published.
1861	Speaks at Massachusetts Anti-Slavery Society.
1862	Lectures in Washington, D.C. Death of Thoreau.
1863	Death of Aunt Mary Moody Emerson. Lectures in the Midwest.
1864	Lectures on "American Life" and "The Fortune of the Republic."

1865	Eulogizes Abraham Lincoln. Delivers seventy-seven lectures.
1866	Receives honorary Doctor of Laws degree from Harvard.
1867	Publishes *May-Day and Other Pieces.* Named an overseer at Harvard.
	Lectures eighty times, traveling as far as Minnesota and Iowa.
1868	Brother William dies in New York.
1869	*Society and Solitude* published. Lectures at Harvard.
1871	Travels to the West Coast. Meets John Muir.
1872	Health problems. Concord home badly damaged by fire. Travels to Egypt and Europe with daughter Ellen.
1873	Returns home to find that the house has been rebuilt by friends.
1875	*Letters and Social Aims* published.
1876–82	Physical and mental decline. Dies of pneumonia April 27, 1882, in Concord.

EMERSON RESOURCES

Writings and Anthologies

Andrews, Barry M., ed. *A Dream Too Wild: Emerson Meditations for Every Day of the Year*. Boston: Skinner House Books, 2003.

Atkinson, Brooks, ed. *The Essential Writings of Ralph Waldo Emerson*. New York: Modern Library, 2000.

Bode, Carl, ed. *The Portable Emerson*. New York: Penguin Books, 1984.

Emerson, Edward Waldo, ed. *The Complete Works of Ralph Waldo Emerson*, 12 vols. Boston: Houghton Mifflin, 1903.

————, and Waldo Emerson Forbes, eds. *The Journals of Ralph Waldo Emerson*, 10 vols. Boston: Houghton Mifflin, 1910.

Gilman, William H., et al., eds. *The Journals and Miscellaneous Notebooks of Ralph Waldo Emerson*, 16 vols. Cambridge, MA: Harvard University Press, 1960–82.

Porte, Joel, ed. *Emerson: Essays and Lectures*. New York: The Library of America, 1983.

————, and Saundra Morris, eds. *Emerson's Prose and Poetry*. New York: W.W. Norton and Co., 2001.

Robinson, David, ed. *The Spiritual Emerson*. Boston: Beacon Press, 2003.

Rusk, Ralph L., and Eleanor Tilden, eds. *The Letters of Ralph Waldo Emerson*, 8 vols. to date. New York: Columbia University Press, 1939–.

Spiller, Robert E., Stephen E. Whicher, and Wallace E. Williams, eds. *The Early Lectures of Ralph Waldo Emerson*, 3 vols. Cambridge, MA: Harvard University Press, 1959–72.

Biographies and Historical and Critical Studies

Boller, Paul E. *American Transcendentalism, 1830–1860: An Intellectual Inquiry*. New York: G.P. Putnam's Sons, 1974.

Dewey, John. "Ralph Waldo Emerson," in Milton R. Konvitz and Stephen E. Whicher, eds., *Emerson: A Collection of Critical Essays*. Englewood Cliffs, NJ: Prentice-Hall, 1962.

Geldard, Richard G. *God in Concord: Ralph Waldo Emerson's Awakening to the Infinite*. Burdette, NY: Larson Publications, 1999.

Myerson, Joel, ed. *A Historical Guide to Ralph Waldo Emerson*. New York: Oxford University Press, 2000.

Paramananda, Swami. *Emerson and Vedanta*. Cohasset, MA: Vedanta Centre Publishers, 1985.

Parker, Theodore. "The Writings of Ralph Waldo Emerson," in Joel Myerson, ed., *Emerson and Thoreau: The Contemporary Reviews*. New York: Cambridge University Press, 1992.

Peabody, Elizabeth. "Emerson as Preacher," in F. B. Sanborn, ed., *The Genius and Character of Emerson*. Port Washington, NY: Kennikat Press, 1971.

Richardson, Robert D., Jr. *Emerson: The Mind on Fire*. Berkeley: University of California Press, 1995.

Robinson, David. *Emerson and the Conduct of Life*. New York: Cambridge University Press, 1993.

Internet Resources

http://www.emersoncentral.com
Emerson texts, site search, research. Visitors may also pose questions, discuss texts, and add their thoughts. Especially suited to high school students. Linked to sister site, transcendentalists.com. See below.

http://www.rwe.org
"The Words of Ralph Waldo Emerson." Includes extensive lists of essays, poems, and addresses; bibliography; images; biography; and time-line. Also has a list of study groups and Emerson bicentennial events.

http://www.transcendentalists.com (also *www.vcu.edu/engweb/*
transcendentalism)
Scholarly website featuring papers, discussions, and links relating to Transcendentalist authors and texts, roots and influences, ideas and thought, criticism and resources.

http://www.walden.org (also *www.freereligion.com*)
Topics include Emerson, Transcendentalism, and other Transcendentalists such as Henry David Thoreau. Site contains original content as well as links to other sites. Features Emerson texts, criticism, quotes, and discussions.

FOR FURTHER READING

Andrews, Barry M., *Thoreau as Spiritual Guide*. Boston: Skinner House Books, 2000.

———. *True Harvest: Readings from Henry David Thoreau for Every Day of the Year*. Boston: Skinner House Books, 2005.

Bridges, William. *The Way of Transition: Embracing Life's Most Difficult Moments*. Cambridge, MA: Perseus Publishing, 2001.

Campbell, Joseph. *The Power of Myth*. New York: Doubleday, 1988.

Carlson, Richard, and Benjamin Shield. *Handbook for the Soul*. Boston: Little, Brown and Co., 1995.

Csikszentmihalyi, Michael. *Flow: The Psychology of Ultimate Experience*. New York: Harper and Row, 1990.

Fox, Matthew. *Creation Spirituality*. San Francisco: HarperSanFrancisco, 1991.

Fulghum, Robert. *It Was on Fire When I Lay Down on It*. New York: Villard Books, 1989.

James, William. *The Varieties of Religious Experience: A Study in Human Nature*. New York: Longmans, Green and Company, 1925.

Kornfield, Jack. *After the Ecstasy, the Laundry*. New York: Bantam Books, 2000.

————. *The Art of Forgiveness, Lovingkindness, and Peace*. New York: Bantam Books, 2002.

Lesser, Elizabeth. *The New American Spirituality: A Seeker's Guide*. New York: Random House, 1999.

McGraw, Philip C. *Self Matters: Creating Your Life from the Inside Out*. New York: Simon and Schuster, 2001.

Moore, Thomas, ed. *The Education of the Heart*. New York: Harper-Collins, 1997.

Palmer, Parker J. *Let Your Life Speak: Listening for the Voice of Vocation*. San Francisco: Jossey-Bass, 2000.

Roof, Wade Clark. *Spiritual Marketplace: Baby Boomers and the Remaking of American Religion*. Princeton, NJ: Princeton University Press, 1999.

Sanders, Scott Russell. *Hunting for Hope*. Boston: Beacon Press, 1998.

Schweitzer, Albert. *An Anthology*, Charles R. Joy, ed. Boston: Beacon Press, 1947.

Smith, Huston. *The World's Religions: Our Great Wisdom Traditions*. New York: HarperCollins, 1991.

Thoreau, Henry David. *Walden*. Boston: Houghton Mifflin, 1906.

Watts, Alan. *TAO: The Watercourse Way*. New York: Pantheon Books, 1975.

Wuthnow, Robert. *After Heaven: Spirituality in America Since the 1950s*. Berkeley: University of California Press, 1998.